## AUTHOR'S PREFACE

Here at long last, is the story of "Margot, the Cobbler." It is the very story which the General of the Cops misconstrued to accuse the author of high treason. The entire army of Parisian prostitutes and their pimps abetted the General in this distortion of the truth. Since the author has been accused of having attacked religion, the government and the King himself in this story, he could not afford to keep silent and thus virtually admit to any guilt. Therefore, the story is being published so that the readers may judge for themselves where lies the right and the wrong.

# CHAPTER ONE. *AT HOME*

It is not because of vanity, and even less out of modesty, that I expose openly the various roles I played when I was young. It is my honest desire—if at all possible—to debase the egotism of those who have searched for a moderate fortune in ways similar to my own. And, above all, I want to offer the public a glowing testimony of my gratitude with the admission that everything I own is the direct result of their generosity and charity.

I was born in the *rue Saint-Paul;* my existence is the result of the furtive liaison between an honorable soldier of the guards and a mender of shoes. My mother, who would rather spend her time on her back, taught me the trade of mending and patching—especially shoes—at a very early age, to rid herself of the responsibility of taking care of me as quickly as she possibly could. I was about thirteen years old when my mother decided that she could leave me her mending coop and her customers, provided of course that she would get her share of my daily take.

I fulfilled her hopes so well that it took me only a very short time before I had become a pearl among the menders in our neighborhood. But I did not limit my talents to cobbling because I was also very adept at patching old trousers and mending the seats. Added to my dexterity and greatly enhancing my business was my charming face with which Nature had graced me. There was nobody in the entire neighborhood who did not want to be waited on by me. My mending coop was the gathering point of all the lackeys of the *rue Saint-Antoine.* Thus, I was continuously exposed to fine company, which gave me my first veneer of good manners and breeding.

My parents had given me, through lineage and good example, such a strong inclination to taste voluptuous pleasures that the desire to walk in their footsteps and try out the sweetness of carnal knowledge almost killed me.

My father, Monsieur Tranche-montagne, my mother and I lived in a single room on the fourth floor. It was furnished with a couple of wicker chairs, an old cupboard with some dirty earthenware dishes, and one wide, miserable bed without curtains and without a blanket upon which the three of us had to sleep.

The older I became the more frequently I awoke during the night because I started to notice the distinct motions of my bed companions. Quite often they were so exuberant that the springs of the bedstead forced me to participate in all of their movements. They were both panting and whispering words of endearment to each other that were dictated by their passion. I suffered unbearable excitement. I was consumed by a smoldering fire which almost took my breath away. At those moments I would have loved to kick and punch my own mother because I was so jealous of the ecstasies she enjoyed. What else could I do when I was plagued by these emotions than resort to the silent lusts of the lonely? It was a blessing that on top of these pressing needs I did not suffer from a cramp in my fingertips. But, alas, what a miserable remedy when compared to the real thing! It was really child's play. I stimulated and wore myself out to no avail and the only result was that I would be more fervent, passionate and frantic than before. I was almost consumed by rage and passion; briefly I wished I could be ravaged by a satyr. A nice disposition for a fourteen-year-old girl but, as the saying goes, I was "a chip off the old block."

One might well understand how this eternally torturing thorn in my flesh caused me to think seriously about procuring some good solid boy friend who might be able to slake this unbearable thirst which made my tongue stick to the roof of my mouth. Or at least some person who might be able to bring about some relief!

# CHAPTER TWO. *PIERROT*

Among the many manservants who continually paid me their compliments was a handsome, robust young groom who rated my special attention. His off-the-cuff compliments were always in the special language of his profession and he claimed that he never rubbed down his charger without thinking about me. Whereupon I would answer that I never worked on a pair of trousers that did not remind me of Monsieur Pierrot (that was his name). We were quite serious and paid each other many other similar compliments in elegantly turned phrases which I can no longer remember. It is enough, dear reader, for you to know that Pierrot and I quickly came to an agreement and a few days later we were to seal our covenant in the back room of a local tavern upon the altar of Venus.

The place of this sacrifice was furnished with an old table and half a dozen chairs that had fallen into decay. The walls were covered with indecent scribblings as is the custom of love-sick couples when they are in a good mood. Our banquet was entirely in keeping with the simplicity of our place of consecration. A small jug of wine for eight pennies, cheese for two and some bread—the entire amount, after careful calculation, was not more than twelve pennies. Nevertheless we celebrated our High Mass with such pleasure as if we had feasted for a gold louis per person at the famous Dupare Inn. One does not have to be surprised at this. Even the coarsest meal becomes a repast when love is a guest.

Finally we had finished. Next we had to solve the difficult problem of how we could make ourselves more comfortable. We were smart enough not to trust either the table or any of the available chairs, so we selected the only remaining possibility: trying to do it standing up. Pierrot made me recline against the wall. Oh, powerful god of the fields! It scared me when I looked down upon what he showed me. Those thrusts! What an attack! The wall creaked and moaned under his monstrous assault. I had made up my mind (because I did not want to have to reproach myself later) that this poor boy was not going to be the only one to suffer from exhaustion after so much hard work. But despite these good intentions, our perseverance and mutual courage, we still had not even made fair to middling progress, and personally I had begun to have my doubts as to whether we were ever going to be able to crown our efforts with some sort of achievement. Then Pierrot got the marvelous idea to wet his enormous tool with some spittle. Oh, Nature, Nature! How marvelous are thy many secrets! The hiding place of love opened itself and he penetrated . . . what more should I say? I was good and thoroughly—as it should be—deflowered.

From that time on I slept much better. Thousands of flattering dreams ruled my sleep. Monsieur and Madame Tranche-montagne could make the bed groan as loudly as they wanted during their amorous entanglements ... I no longer heard them.

Our innocent love affair lasted for almost a year. I adored Pierrot and he loved me. He was quite a man indeed, whose only fault was his continuous lack of money. And since among good friends the rich help the poor, it was I who had to supply him with whatever he needed to pay for his expenses. Though the proverb states that a true cavalier would rather eat his stirrups than accept support from a lady, my boy friend, to the contrary, consumed the proceeds of my business because he loved to drink and gamble and obviously wanted to spare his stirrups. Soon I was even forced to sell my mending coop.

My mother had long since noticed that my business had fallen off sharply and she reproached me sternly. To make things worse, she soon learned from gossip in the neighborhood that my innocence had been thoroughly ruined. But, dear mother did not say anything about that. However, one morning, when I was still in a deep sleep, she armed herself with a brand new cane, and after she had sneakily pulled my nightshirt over my head, she set my buttocks afire before I had a chance to defend myself. Just imagine the incredible humiliation for a grown girl to wake up being punished like that! I was so furious that I decided right then and there to become independent and try to make my own living as I saw fit. And since I had made up my mind, I waited for an opportunity when my mother would be out of the house. I quickly put on my Sunday finery and said goodbye forever to the home of my mother.

# CHAPTER THREE. *NEW ACQUAINTANCE*

I walked around at random and finally arrived at the *place Greve;* from there I walked along the banks of the Seine toward the *Tuileries.* I strolled aimlessly about the gardens without giving any thought to what I was going to do. By the time I had calmed down a little I had arrived at the *Terrasses des Capucins.* I sat there for more than a half hour, thinking about what to do next, when a smartly dressed lady of excellent demeanor sat down next to me. We nodded and started one of those conversations that people often do when they like to talk but actually have nothing of importance to say.

"Oh, Mademoiselle, isn't it hot today?"

"Terribly hot, Madame."

"Fortunately there is a slight breeze."

"Yes, Madame, a little."

"Oh, Mademoiselle, can you imagine when the weather stays this way how many people will go to *Saint-Cloud!"*

"I am sure, Madame, there will be many."

"Ah, Mademoiselle, the longer I look at you, the more I am convinced that we have met. Didn't I have the pleasure of seeing you in Bretagne?"

"Oh, no, Madame, I have never been outside of Paris."

"Well, you look exactly like a young lady I know from Nantes, Mademoiselle. You two could easily be mistaken for one another. I assure you that this in no way is an insult to you, because she is one of the loveliest maidens I have ever seen."

"You are too kind, Madame; I know that I am not lovely at all. It is only your kindness that makes you think this. And besides, it would not help me one whit, even if I were lovely."

I underscored my last words with a deep sigh and a few tears welled from my eyes.

"But what is the matter, my dear child?" she said, pressing my hand affectionately. "You are crying! What is it that troubles you? What misfortune has befallen you? Please, do tell me, little one. Don't be ashamed; speak your mind frankly. I have taken a great liking to you and you can be assured that I will do whatever is in my power to help you. Come, my little angel, let us walk to the other side of the *Terrasses* and have some breakfast at Madame La Croix' who owns *le Cafe des Tuileries.* Then you can pour out your heart and 'talk freely about your sorrows. It is quite possible that I can be of much greater help to you than you think."

She did not have to twist my arm after this kindly invitation because my poor stomach was very empty. I followed her, and there was no doubt in my mind that she had been sent to me by Heaven and was going to help me with more than just solid advice. I was sure this kind lady was going to rescue me from the terrible dangers that can befall a lonely girl walking the streets of Paris.

After I had fortified myself with two cups of coffee with cream, and some French rolls, I told her quite frankly about my origin and my profession. I was not as candid about certain other things and I felt it would be more appropriate to heap all the blame upon my mother. For that reason I painted a rather bleak picture of her so that I could justify my reason for having run away from home.

"Holy Mother of God!" exclaimed my benign, unknown benefactress. "The tortures you must have suffered to be forced into such a lowly profession. Imagine, such a charming child, year in, year out, exposed to the weather . . . the heat of the sun, the cold of winter; to be forced to crouch inside a mender's coop and patch up the boots of every passerby. No, my little princess, you were not born to suffer this. Because—and I surely do not have to keep this a secret from you—when one is as pretty as you are, one does not have to perform such menial labors. And I am sure that I could find something much better for you to do, if you are the kind of girl that is willing to take advice and guidance."

"Oh, my dearest lady," I exclaimed, "please do tell me! What should I do? Help me in any way you see fit. I deliver myself entirely into your keeping."

"That is fine," she resumed. "We will live together. I have four other girls *en pension,* and you are going to be the fifth."

"But, Madame," I answered prematurely, "how could I? Have you so soon forgotten that it would be entirely out of the question in my present miserable condition to pay even one single penny for room and board?"

"You do not have to worry about that at all," she smiled. "The only thing I ask of you at this time is your obedience and willingness to accept my guidance. We will handle all other details later. I have a small business proposition and I flatter myself that with God's help you will not only be fully able to repay me but also have enough money to support yourself completely ere this month has ended."

An enormous feeling of gratitude welled up in me and I almost threw myself at her feet and bedewed them with my tears. I felt a great desire to be taken into this blessed little family. Thanks to my lucky stars my impatience was not tried too much.

# CHAPTER FOUR. *THE HOUSE*

It was around noon when we left the *Ter-rasses* through the *Porte-Feuillantine*. A venerable *fiacre* took us in his plush cab and, after the calmly trotting horses had reached the Boulevards, drove us to an isolated home opposite the *rue Montmartre*.

The house looked very secluded, nestled between a courtyard and a garden, and I presumed that the lucky inhabitants of this fine mansion must be very happy and fortunate indeed. Silently I blessed the humiliating circumstances which had awakened me so rudely earlier this morning, since the result had been this remarkable acquaintanceship.

I was led into a beautifully furnished large room on the ground floor, and soon I was introduced to my future companions. Their coquetry, their charming—albeit slightly sloppy—make-up, their resolute manners and their self-assured demeanor frightened me so much at first that I hardly dared look up. I stammered and stuttered when I tried to answer their friendly greetings. My benefactress, who immediately assumed that the simple clothes I was wearing could be the reason for my nervousness, promised me to change my outfit without delay and added that I would soon be just as finely bedecked as these young ladies. Indeed, I did feel slightly humiliated, being among women whose morning robes were made out of the finest Indian and French cloth, since I wore only the frumpy garments of a girl of the working class. But there was one thing which made me very curious and also slightly worried. I wanted to know what sort of a business I was expected to enter. The luxury which my newfound friends obviously could permit themselves surprised me greatly; I was not capable of imagining how they could possibly afford these expenditures. I was so humble, or rather, still so inexperienced, that I did not have the vaguest notion of what was literally forcing itself into my mind. And while I was still trying very hard to think of a solution to this apparent mystery, the soup was served and we seated ourselves at the table. Even though the cooking was bad, we corrected its preparation with a lot of pepper. We ate so much that the kitchen personnel did not get a single table scrap.

So far, everything had gone very well. But when two of the ladies had surpassed the boundaries of moderation and the fumes of Bacchus started to veil their minds, one suddenly punched her fist into the mouth of the other, who in turn revenged herself with a blow in her friend's soup dish. In no time at all the table, the dishes, meat and sauce were spread all over the floor. War had been declared. My two heroines flew at each other with equal animosity. Scarves, bonnets, sleeves, all were tattered in an instance. When the mistress of the house tried to get in between and assert her authority, they pasted her—as if by mistake—in the face with a platter of sauce. Since she was totally unprepared for this peculiar caress and since patience obviously did not belong among her most outstanding virtues, making peace was now out of the question. On the spot she gave a demonstration of her superiority in the heroic art of boxing. Meanwhile, the two others who had so far remained neutral, felt that they could no longer idly stand by, whereupon the entire affair became even more fascinating and an all-out battle ensued.

The moment it all started I had retired to the farthest corner of the room, quaking with fear, and I did not move as long as the brawl lasted. It was a terrifying yet at the same time farcical comedy to see these five creatures tumble over and under each other, biting, scratching, kicking and hitting, simultaneously screaming obscenities at each other and now and then showing in a most unseemly manner their large and small tools of the trade.

**18**

There was no indication that this massacre would be over soon were it not for an old man, who looked as if he had lived in the gutter all his life, announcing the arrival of a German baron. And you know how much respected these personages are among demimondaines; almost as much as the Mylords. The word "baron" had hardly been uttered when the entire battle was over and done with instantly. The amazons separated and hastily tidied their tattered gowns. They dried themselves, dusted one another and the distorted, overheated faces assumed momentarily their tender and natural friendliness. Our mistress left quickly to entertain the baron and the ladies hastened to their rooms to dress appropriately and repair their faces in order to be able to receive him suitably.

The reader, who is undoubtedly more experienced than I was in those days, must have already guessed that I had landed in one of the best-run houses of Paris. And he will also be aware that our gracious hostess was one of the most sought after in this business; she called herself Madame Florence.

As soon as she found out that the arrival of the baron had been announced for the sole purpose of putting an end to the fighting, she walked over to me with a very satisfied and happy expression on her face. She lightly kissed my forehead and said, "Just because of this slight disagreement you witnessed a moment ago, I do not want you to think badly of us, my little one. They were very unimportant differences of opinion about nothing and against nobody in particular. They blow over in a minute. After all, one is not always master of one's emotions. And at such times people's feelings are more or less sensitive. Even the worm wriggles when you step on it. When you get to know the ladies a little bit better, you will be enchanted by their charming dispositions. They truly are the most kind-hearted creatures in all the world. Their fury is like passion—short-

**19**

lived; it dies down as quickly as it flares up. In a minute everything will be forgotten. Thank God that I don't even know how it feels to be vengeful; and I am no more venomous than a turtledove. I feel sorry for those who wish me ill luck, because I surely don't wish it upon anybody. But now we should talk about you.

"You will have to admit, my dear child, that one does not have a chance in today's society when one is not rich. 'No money, no blessings,' is the proverb. But one can also paraphrase and say, 'No money, no pleasures and no comforts in life.' And since it is very simple to appraise comfortable living and other luxuries, I think you will have to agree with me that it would be rather stupid to reject a livelihood, especially if one possesses the means for it and does not do any harm to society. Because that would be very sinful. Yes, my child, may the good Lord protect us. But in this respect I have an absolutely clear conscience and I take careful precautions against any possible accusation. And we are, after all, not among the Turks; we have to think about the salvation of our souls. And, moreover, it is not against the law to earn your living in this or that manner. It is not a question of what profession one takes up. What is important is that you are good at it. As I have already told you, it is rather stupid when one does not use his God-given talents to make a good living as long as one can. And tell me, who could do that better than you, with all the resources good Nature has equipped you? She has certainly not made you so beautiful merely to let it go to waste. I know so many girls who are far less charming and attractive than you who nevertheless manage to make a very fair income. They have discovered the secret! And I may add without bragging that have never taken too much out of their earnings, though their way to riches was entirely my doing. But I pray that the good Lord may have pity upon those ingrates. I don't want to encroach upon their pleasures."

"Oh, my dear, dear lady," again I spoke too quickly. "I hope that you never have to accuse me of such ingratitude."

"Do not commit yourself, my dear," she replied. "They have all said the same thing, and yet they still have completely forgotten me! When fortune smiles upon them, people show their true color. Ah, if you only knew how many girls go to the *Opera* who received their entire education from me and who pretend now that they have never known me, then you would be forced to admit that gratitude is not one of the virtues that is practiced in this profession. But, nevertheless, it is always a great pleasure to find someone who is in need of assistance. By the way, my little pussycat, as young and beautiful as you are, have you never had a suitor?"

"Who? Me, Madame?" I answered in a hypocritical tone of voice. "Who would ever take notice of me in my present deplorable situation?"

"I think you prefer not to understand me," she retorted. "Now you have forced me to be more blunt about it. Are you still a virgin?"

This unexpected question surprised me so much that my cheeks turned blood red and I lost my composure entirely. "I see, you've lost it," she said. "But that is not too important. We have creams that work wonders and we can restore it so that nobody would know the difference. All the young ladies who decide to go into the profession have to undergo a similar examination and treatment. It is merely a ceremony, and it does not hurt at all. You must admit that it is just good business when a merchant knows his wares."

While she was talking, Madame Florence had pulled my skirt high above my waist. She turned me around and looked me over very thoroughly. Nothing escaped her experienced eyes.

"Very good," she said. "I am satisfied. The damage you have suffered is not too great. It can easily be repaired. Thank God you have one of the most beautiful bodies I have ever seen, and you should be able to derive great benefits from it. But one of the most important duties of our profession is not to be stingy with the use of the sponge. And it appears to me that you are totally unfamiliar with this habit. Come with me, and I will show you as long as we still have time."

She led me immediately into a small dressing room and made me straddle over a bidet. She then taught me my first lesson in hygiene. The remainder of the day was spent with her teaching me various other, less important things about my future profession.

# CHAPTER FIVE. *MADAME FLORENCE*

The next morning, as she had promised, Madame Florence changed me from head to toe. She gave me a gown of rose-colored silk taffeta with a furbelow, a muslin chemise and a large gold-colored timepiece for my belt.

I thought I looked simply devastating in my new outfit and since I experienced the pangs of vanity for the first time in my life, I looked upon myself with a mixture of satisfaction, admiration and respect.

One has to give Madame Florence her proper due; she had planned everything down to the most minute detail. Among the abbesses of Cytherea she was truly the greatest genius. She knew the solutions to every problem. Aside from the boarders that were always in her house, she held many girls in the city in reserve just in case business should pick up suddenly; she did not want to be caught shorthanded. Sometimes she had special requests and always knew a girl able to fulfill such. But that was not all; she also had a warehouse stocked with gowns and dresses in various designs and many colors which she loaned to new and destitute beginners like myself. This, too, increased her income considerably.

To be sure that her outlay would quickly bear interest, Madame Florence had already informed some of her best customers of her new find. And because of this sensible precautionary measure we did not have to wait too long. Monsieur President de L . . ., who always showed up promptly the moment he was notified of a new discovery, arrived that night at eleven o'clock sharp, just as I had finished my toilette. I saw a man of medium build, completely dressed in black, standing erect with chin held high. He held his neck stiff, so that when he moved his head, his entire torso turned with it. He wore an artificially coiffed wig which was so heavily powdered with *poudre a la marechale* that three quarters of it covered his jacket. Aside from that, such a heavy smell of ambrosia and musk wafted around this personage that only those who were used to heady perfumes barely managed to keep from fainting.

"Ah, Florence," he exclaimed while staring at me, "that is really something beautiful; truly precious and divine. This time you have outdone yourself. Really, I am serious, *Mademoiselle* is adorable. She is a hundred times more beautiful than you have told me. Upon my honor, she is an angel. I do not exaggerate when I call her a marvelous specimen. Just look at those beautiful eyes! I have to press a kiss upon them; I simply cannot resist."

Madame Florence, who had already foreseen the following events, and who knew that the presence of a third person was superfluous, discreetly retired into another room and left the two of us alone. Without giving up his majestic posture, M. President immediately sat me down upon the couch, and after he had amused himself for a while with touching and looking at my most secret charms, he forced me into a posture which was exactly the opposite to the one I used to take with Pierrot. But, I had been advised to be kind and obliging. I spread my legs while bending over as if to touch my toes, unaware of his ultimate goal. He gripped me tightly about the waist and pushed me even farther forward, so that I almost lost my balance. I was completely helpless in this position. I hoped that he would hurry. A sharp pain in my nether hole announced his attack, and I struggled to rise, or at least to correct what I believed to be his faulty aim. But to no avail. The perfidious gentleman did to me what all debauchees dream of doing and I lost my second virginity. My convulsive movements during this unnatural operation, and the loud screams that escaped me against my will, made it clear to M. President that I did not share his passionate ardor at all. To compensate me, and also to make me forget the pains I had suffered, he pressed two *louis d'or* into my hands.

"This is in addition to your regular fee," he stated, "and you do not have to tell Madame Florence about it. I take care of all the fees, including yours. Fare-thee-well, my little queen, but first I want to press one more kiss upon your adorable, tiny orifice. So! I hope we will meet again during the next few days. Yes, we will have to see each other again because I am greatly satisfied with you and the way you have behaved yourself."

Upon those words he left the room with quick small steps. The floorboards of the room creaked because he walked on the tips of his toes and kept his knees stiff. I did not understand in the least what had happened to me and I did not know at all what to think. Either M. President had made a mistake or this peculiar way of taking possession of an innocent girl must be the habit of people of a certain rank and position. Well, if that happens to be the fashion, I told myself, I suppose I have to get used to it. I am not more sensitive than anybody else. Any new method that is tried out for the first time can be rather exhausting. But, after all, there is nothing to which one cannot get used to in time. I had become rather accustomed to Pierrot's methods, though in the beginning I had to strain myself to get used to him.

I was still engrossed in this interesting conversation with myself when Madame Florence entered the room again.

"Well, young lady," she said, rubbing her hands, "don't you think M. President has a charming personality? Did he give you anything?"

"No, Madame," I answered.

"Look here," she countered, "this is a *louis d'or*. He has ordered me to give this gold piece to you. I hope it will not remain the only token of his great appreciation for you, because he seemed to be extremely satisfied with your services. Please, don't think, my dear child, that all our devotions are so simple or for that matter so richly rewarded. As with every business there are losses and there are gains. The pleasures make up for the disappointments. There is not a single merchant who makes good money all the time. One has to take the gains and the losses with equal good graces. Our profession would be a true goldmine were it not for the fact that we also have to put up with some bad customers. But, never lose your patience. Soon the esteemed members of the clergy will have their conventions. I entertain high hopes that you will then see the money virtually roll into our coffers. Truly—and I don't want to sound vain—my house does not have a bad name. If I had as many thousands in income as I have received prelates, abbots and other high-ranking gentlemen, I would be able to live like a queen. Mind you, I would not be justified if I seem to complain. The Lord has been very good to me and I could stop working right now. But, whosoever is of no use to himself, is of no use to anybody. And, besides, a person has to have *some* form of occupation. 'Idleness is the root of all evil,' as the proverb says. If everyone were to stick to his business, we would have no troubles in this world."

While Madame Florence was flooding me with her boring sagacities and proverbs, I almost got a cramp in my jaw from trying to stifle a compulsive yawning. She finally noticed it and sent me up to my room, reminding me to be sure and make good use of the bidet.

I cannot help myself, but as a sort of marginal note I would like to state that the respectable ladies are greatly indebted to us. Not only do they have us to thank for this useful piece of furniture, but for many other inventions that make life more pleasurable, as well as for the art of enhancing or repairing the natural charms and hiding certain blemishes from prying eyes. It is we who taught them the secrets of multiplying their charms and how to employ them to their fullest extent, to dress up and use ornaments, and above all they learned from our demeanor and our behavior. These are the many things that have excited their curiosity, because it is from us that they copy their latest fashions and notions whose charms are very difficult to define. Briefly, it is easy to gossip about us. But respectable women will only be considered worthy of adoring as long as they can imitate us, when their virtue is ever so slightly tainted with the smell of sin and when they understand how to play the game of coquetry and assume a frivolous character. If only it were possible that this fictitious disparity could be uncovered to restore our good reputation and force out the stereotyped prejudice, and above all rescue our honor!

But I will resume my story. Madame Florence, who had so vociferously spoken out against idleness, did not leave me much time for melancholy thoughts. She brought me quickly back to reality.

"My dear heart," she said lovingly. "I really hesitate to trouble you so quickly. But your friends are downstairs, busily occupied with a bunch of frivolous soldiers. To introduce you to them would truly have bothered my conscience; they pay very badly and I have no intention of employing your abilities for free. Downstairs is a farmer who is a friend of mine. He is an old customer who brings me two *louis d'or* every week as sure as night follows day. And of all people, I would not want to appear unaccommodating toward him. What do you think, little girl? Two *louis d'or* is nothing to sneeze at, especially not when it is so easily earned."

"It is not as easy as you think it is, Madame," I answered. "If you had to suffer yourself what I just went through (I still felt pretty sore) . . ."

"Oh, but no one is as horrible as that man!" she interrupted. "What I am proposing now is just a little game, nothing else. I guarantee you that his caresses are neither long-lasting nor exhausting. With him, the whole thing is over and done with in a very short while."

After Madame Florence had finally succeeded in getting my permission, she introduced me to the most boring tax collector type one can imagine. Just try to picture this: a huge bald head, halfway hidden between the broad shoulders of a weight lifter; staring mean-looking eyes overshadowed by bushy reddish eyebrows; a low wrinkled forehead; a fat triple chin; a heavy drinker's belly; and the whole thing supported by short, heavy bowlegs with flat feet that would do honor to a gander. All these small traits, every single one in its proper place, betrayed the revenue man. I was so surprised at the sight of this creature that I did not even notice how our hostess quietly absented herself.

"Well," said the tax collector in a brutal tone of voice, "did we get together to stand in front of each other with our arms crossed? You are standing there as rigid as a beanpole! Come on, come on, dammit! Come here, girl! I have no time for a quiet *tete-a-tete* because I am due at a meeting shortly. So, let's get it over with. Where are your hands. Give them to me. Good God, what a fumbler! Quick, put your fingers around it. Now, up and down . . . loosely from the wrist! That's it ... yes ... right . a little bit stronger . . . Stop! . . . Now, quicker . . . Careful! Yes ... yes, that's very good . . .'

Suddenly my hands were covered with his sticky white tribute to my skill in following commands.

This pleasant exercise was hardly finished when he threw a few coins in my direction and disappeared as quickly as if his creditors were chasing him.

When I thought about the strange and horrible demands that are expected from a demi-mondaine, I really did not know if I could think of any service that is more miserable and loathsome. And I exclude neither the galley slave nor the courtier. Can there truly be anything more unbearable than to be forced to satisfy the lusts of any man who happens to come along? To smile lovingly at some depraved rogue whom one loathes with every fiber of one's being? To make love to the object of general repulsion? To submit continually to acts which are as strange as they are unnatural? In a word: to hide behind a mask of artistic skill and hypocrisy; to laugh, sing and drink; to commit every imaginable kind of excess and aberration, while the mind is filled with horror and deepest repulsion. How miserably informed are those who think that our lives consist of one string of uninterrupted joy and pleasure! All the crawling and despicable slaves who live in the courts of this world and who can only maintain their positions by suffering uncounted humiliations, submissive servility and continuous hypocrisy, still don't suffer half as much disappointment or undergo as many humiliations as the girls of our profession. It is not at all difficult for me to make the following statement: if our suffering were to be considered a merit and would be counted as penance for our deeds in this world, there would hardly be one among us who would not have her place in the histories of the martyrs or be worthy of canonization. Although a miserable desire for money may have been the motive for our prostitution, the oppressive general contempt, the outrageous humiliation and the insults we have to suffer are more than fair punishment for it. One must have been a whore to fully understand the terror of this trade. It is not without shuddering that I am trying to remember the hardships I had to endure during my apprenticeship. And still I must admit: how many are there who have suffered far more than I? Maybe that one who is driven around triumphantly in a golden, charmingly painted coach, laquered by *Martin,* that one—I dare say—who displays an almost revolting luxury matching the perverted and filthy taste of her benefactor. Who would believe that she is considered to be the meanest among the servants, that this

29

same person is the pitiful object of the arrogance, wantonness and brutality of the meanest *canaille,* in short, that she may still bear the visible marks of physical punishment? I repeat: everything that seems pleasant and alluring in our profession is but illusion and far from the truth. There *is* nothing more humiliating, nothing more terrifying.

One cannot imagine—unless one knows from bitter experience—the excesses and aberrations of which many men are capable when they are caught in the delirium of their passions. I have known many who received their most voluptuous pleasures by being whipped, or who derived the same ecstasy from whipping another, and it has often happened that I was forced—after I had thoroughly whipped or boxed someone black and blue—to undergo similar tortures. It must seem simply amazing that there are always girls available who endure such a way of life patiently.

But it is amazing what the taste of lasciviousness, avarice, sloth and the hope of a happy future can bring about in people.

During the nearly four months that I stayed at Madame Florence's house, I may pride myself that I went through the most complete course on how to become a woman of pleasure. And when I left this excellent school I possessed all the skill and dexterity necessary to satisfy the old-fashioned and modern ways of lust, to bring about artful variations in the release of passion and to be fully conversant in every thinkable form of gymnastics in the field of lechery and fornication.

A small adventure which went beyond the limits of my endurance made me decide to start working on my own account and to live by myself. It happened as follows:

One day we were visited by an entire band of soldiers whose passions were as hot as their purses were empty. They had liberally sacrificed to Bacchus and thereupon decided to bestow their adoration upon the ladies of Venus.

Unfortunately, only two of us were at the house at that time. And to make it worse, my colleague was taking a cure with a strengthening medicine which tempered her ardor and made it temporarily impossible for her to be of any use to these visiting gentlemen. Thus I was left completely alone with them. In vain I tried to respectfully point out to them that it was absolutely impossible to properly satisfy the demands of so many people at once. But, whether I wanted to or not, I had to do whatever they desired. Finally I had to endure thirty attacks within two hours. Oh, how T wished that some devout ladies would have wanted to take my place and undergo the brutal treatment I received so they might have worked toward the redemption of their eternal souls! But as far as I, miserable sinner, am concerned, I have to admit that it was far from me to endure this entire affair patiently and to top if off with a Christian blessing for my rapists. I did not cease during this entire scene to heap the most incredible blasphemies upon their heads. After all, too much is too much. I was so gorged with sensual delights that I was no longer capable of digesting them.

# CHAPTER SIX. *A HOME OF MY OWN*

After this vulgar and brutal visitation it was clear, even to Madame Florence, that it was useless to try and talk me into staying at the house any longer. She agreed to our separation with the condition that I would be available to render my services whenever the house needed extra help. And thus we said our farewells with mutual understanding and respect. I bought a few pieces of furniture with which I decorated a small home in the *rue d'Argen-teuil* and believed that I had succeeded in escaping police supervision. But what is the use of human cunning when fate has decided against us? Jealous, wrongful accusations disturbed the peace of my seclusion and disrupted my carefully laid plans just when I least expected it.

Among the shameless debauchees that secretly visited me was one who, whilst in a very bad humor, tried to make me responsible for a certain very critical indisposition he had suddenly contracted. I arrogantly listened to his wild accusations. His rantings became louder and louder and he treated me in such a shameful manner that two or three whores in the neighborhood who were very jealous of my success ran to the police and blackened my reputation. They were so successful that I was picked up and carted off to *Bicetre*.

The first ceremony to which I had to submit myself consisted of an examination with more than the necessary touching and feeling by four or five medical students at *Saint-Come*. They decided unanimously that I had spoiled blood and they condemned me to undergo immediately and without contradiction a sanitation experiment. *Hie et nunc;* here and now. After I had been properly prepared, which means I was given a bloodletting, an enema and a bath, I was rubbed all over with that certain powerful greasiness in which many globules are suspended that divide and thin out the lymphatic fluids by their activity and heaviness and thus restore the natural flow.

One does not have to be surprised that I am so conversant with the professional terminology. I had plenty of time to learn them all during the more than a month I spent with those blood cleansers. And, moreover, is there anything about which we pleasure girls are not able to talk since we have received our education from the public? Is there any profession or trade or craft about which we don't have the constant opportunity to hear conversation? The warrior, the lawyer, the financier, the philosopher and the man of the cloth . . . all these people try to do business with us in the same time-honored manner. And every one of them speaks the special language of his class. How is it possible to become well educated by so many means and then to pass up the opportunity? I don't know.

During my stay at *Bicetre* I had the honor to make the acquaintance of several *demoiselles* whose names I would not dare mention for fear of incurring the wrath of some of the highest ranking men in the kingdom whose idols these girls had become. There are personages that have to be respected despite the depravity of their inclinations. It is not fitting for us to criticize the way of life of the great men of the world. When they prefer to consort with abject, base, vile and despicable people rather than pay their respects to those who deserve to be honored by everyone and those who possess cultivated sentiments, that is their business.

Every time I was outside in the water basin of *Saint-Come* I was gripped by the intense desire to run away from my imprisonment. I wrote to all my influential friends in the most ingratiating manner begging them to do their utmost to try to achieve my release. But my letters never reached them, or rather, my friends pretended that they had never received them. I was desperate at the thought that all of them let me sit there. Then I suddenly thought about M. President de L . . ., the one who had 'deflowered' me in such an unnatural manner. I begged him to help me and my pleas were not without results. Four days after I had sent my letter I was told that I was free to go. I was so overcome with joy and filled with such intense gratitude for the great service which this magnanimous High Justice rendered me, that it would have greatly pleased me to sacrifice twenty more of my virginities, and each one of them better than its predecessor, he had expressed such a desire.

When I returned to society I could have ended more than ever before upon my harms. It seemed as if the medicine that flowed through my veins had made an entirely different being out of me. I had become a breathtaking beauty though I still lacked one important ingredient. I knew next to nothing about those indefinable secrets which would bring out the advantages Nature had given me with the help of art and cosmetics. I was truly stupid and I believed that a nice complexion, a pleasant facial expression and a good figure were enough to be pleasing. Completely inexperienced and without any knowledge of certain tricks and little frauds the fairer sex employs, I left it up to my pretty face to supply myself with admirers. But I did not draw a single glance. On the contrary, I had to suffer the indignity of being pushed into the background by faces that were tainted with debauchery, thickly covered with white and red make-up, and since I did not want to run the risk of sinking back into the gutter out of which I had so recently crawled, I was forced to become a painter's model in order to earn a livelihood.

During the six months that I carried on this beautiful trade, I had the honor to be the object of studies and of recreation for practically every dauber and paint dribbler in Paris. There was hardly any profane or sacred subject for which I had not posed. Now I was portrayed as a penitent

Magdalene, then I was Pasiphae about to conceive by a white bull. Today I would be a Saint and tomorrow a whore, completely depending upon the mood of these gentlemen or upon the commission they had received. But even though I possessed one of the most beautiful and well-built bodies, a laundress by the name of Marguerite—who now calls herself *Mademoiselle Jolie*—suddenly got the better of me and took all my clients away. The reason for this was that my body had become thoroughly known and Marguerite, though she was in every respect inferior to me, was a novelty. Nevertheless, whatever charms she possessed did not come out in the portraits as well as the painters had hoped for. She was so incredibly lively that it was near to impossible to contain her in any particular pose. She had to be caught, so to say, in flight. One of her indiscreet pranks so truly characteristic of her, was the following:

One day, Monsieur T . . . painted her as "Chaste Susanna," which means she did not wear a stitch of clothes. He had to leave his studio for a moment and just about the same time a procession of barefoot penitent monks came by. The foolish girl completely forgot about her state of undress and rushed onto the balcony displaying all her charms in a rather unseemly manner. The people out in the street who became far more excited about the indecency of her behavior than the gentlemen of the Church, greeted Marguerite with a hail of stones. This adventure almost had terrible consequences for poor Monsieur T. . . . They insisted upon accusing him of being an accessory to the crime. Fortunately he got away with excommunication only.

# CHAPTER SEVEN. *MONSIEUR DE MEZ .*

Meanwhile, the reputation Marguerite gained every day in our mutual profession, caused me to accept the suggestion of a soldier to become his boarder for one hundred francs per month. Monsieur de Mez . . . (this was the name of my protector) loved me to the point of adoration. I loved him just as much, which is considered an exceptional phenomenon among kept girls, because usually an unconquerable feeling of disgust is the reward for the man who keeps a mistress. However it might have been, I certainly did not swear eternal fidelity and I did not have to keep myself available for him alone. A young wigmaker and a broad-shouldered baker's journeyman took turns acting as a substitute for him. The first one could enter my room any time he pleased under the pretense of having to coif me, and the other gained the same rights by claiming to bring me my bread, without ever causing Monsieur de Mez ... to entertain the slightest shadow of a doubt.

Everything seemed to work together to give me the greatest happiness. If fate had supplied me nicely with all the necessities, love gave me more than my salacious desires needed. I had every reason to be very content with my position. And I really was, till a confounded mix-up brought nothing but wild confusion into our little household. The court had been transferred to *Fontainebleau* and Monsieur de Mez . . . belonged to the detachment and had to stay in his quarters throughout the duration of the journey. My landlady, who counted upon his absence, asked me to give up my room for a private party and his wife who wanted to stay in Paris for a couple of days. I did not want to embarrass the dear lady and agreed to her request. We decided to sleep in her room as long as the two strangers used my bed. And that same evening those two good people took up lodging in my room in the hope that they could recoup some of their strength which they had lost during the many sleepless nights of their journey.

Monsieur de Mez . . ., who was obviously driven by a deep desire to spend the night with me, arrived at just about the time when we all had fallen asleep. He had the keys to the house and to the room. He entered very quietly, but his gentle soul was shaken to its very foundation when he heard a sonorous loud snoring. Overcome with fury he tiptoed toward my bed. Fumbling, he felt . . . *two* heads! Suddenly the demon of jealousy and the spirit of wrath took possession of his mind and he attacked the sleeping couple with terrible blows from his walking cane. He broke the arm of the poor devil of a husband who tried to protect his better half from this sudden onslaught. One can well imagine that this scene did not exactly unfold in deepest silence. Soon the entire household and neighborhood were awakened by the terrified screams of the unlucky couple. Everyone cried out, "Murder!" "Thieves!" Soon the guards arrived and Monsieur de Mez . . ., who discovered his mistake too late, was arrested and taken to the City Hall. Since the whole uproar had broken out on account of me, I did not deem it advisable to remain and wait what turn the whole affair was going to take. I quickly grabbed my underwear and threw a house dress over my shoulders, and fled under the protection of the general turmoil to the home of the canon of the *Saint-Nicolas* church.

# CHAPTER EIGHT. *THE CANON*

It had taken quite a while before this devout man had shown any desire for me. God knows, maybe it irritated him to find such a beautiful opportunity to release the lewdness which burned him up. However, he received me in a very Christian manner. And after he had made me drink a glass of delicious *aquavit,* from which he had also taken a hearty draught to appease his conscience, the old libertine laid me charitably in his canonical bed. It is certainly not without good reason that the particular talents of these eaters of Holy Water soup are so widely renowned. Compared to them, secular people are just plain, stunted, miserable wretches. That worthy priest performed, throughout the night and well into the day, true miracles of Nature. Whenever he threatened to wear out and be overcome with exhaustion, sheer desire made him go to pieces and his voluptuous fantasies—which were endless—gave him unending vigor. Every single area of my body was for him the object of adoration, devotion and sacrifice. Neither the writings of Aretino nor the immodest paintings of Clinchtel, despite the knowledge these gentlemen possessed, would have been capable f inventing even half of all the postures and positions into which the canon forced me.

The occasion did give me the opportunity though to become fully intimate with the canon, and he offered to share the fruits of his maintenance with me which, to tell the truth, were not too large. But the distressing situation in which I found myself did not allow me to be too choosy and so I accepted his offer wholeheartedly.

That same evening, at dusk, he loaned me an old pair of trousers in which his venerable reproductive tools must have dangled for at least ten years. And after he had thrown an old short cassock of about the same age around me and made me put on a woolen jacket with holes in it and bands under my chin, we left the house without being challenged; without anybody even talking to us. The devil himself would not have recognized me in this farcical disguise. My girl's figure was hidden so completely that I looked less like a woman and more like one of those poverty-stricken, pockmarked Irishmen who earn their livelihood by celebrating Masses.

Dear reader, you will never guess whereto my new lord and master brought me: to the *rue Champ-fleuri,* up to the fifth floor where a woman named Thomas lived who dealt in old hats. A few years ago this venerable old lady had been the canon's housekeeper. She had left him to marry a water vendor who lived in this *quartier.* However, that poor man did not need much time to exchange this life for a better one soon after the wedding ceremonies. And since he did not leave the widow Thomas much more than the fog of the river which had been his only means of livelihood, the lady had become a member of the guild of secondhand dealers. My priest left me in the of this honorable burgess for the time being till he would be able to find a suitable hideout for us.

Madame Thomas was a strong, pug-nosed, fairly heavily built woman. Nevertheless, one could detect, despite her massive fullness, that once upon a time she had possessed a figure which made men take notice of her. The dear little old woman had a secret affair going with a mendicant friar of the seraphim order of St. Francis. He paid homage to her charms whenever the stimulus of the flesh became unbearable to her.

It is incomprehensible how fate uses peculiar means to work miracles and guide us poor mortals along the path which we are destined to walk. Could anyone ever get the notion that the imaginative God reached me with his blessings in the home of an old female dealer in secondhand hats? Yet nothing is more true than that.

Brother Alexis raised me up out of the dust and became the first source of the abundance which I enjoy today. But what is even more surprising, and eludes our mere human understanding, is that the chain of events which opens the gates of happiness is so frequently linked with unpleasant happenings. For instance: a poor stranger who feels completely secure in my bedroom gets caned so unmercifully that he breaks his arm. Because I am afraid that I will be held responsible for this tragic incident I flee to my neighbor, the canon of the cathedral, who brings me to the home of Madame Thomas. But that is not the last of it. Aside from the ill luck I just mentioned, I hear the next day that the dealer in simony was killed by the fragments of his own church and buried under the ruins. And because of this unexpected death I gain a place of refuge without any strings attached thanks to my new landlady.

The confusing emotions caused by my present situation released a flood of tears from which Madame Thomas assumed I mourned the dear departed. Thereupon we cried together for a few minutes. But then the good woman, who was a natural enemy of woe and sorrow, tried to console me. And she was more successful with her quaint suggestions than any doctor would have been with all the pathos of Christian morality.

"Come on now, *Mademoiselle,* keep your chin up," she said. "Now you have to use your head. Even if we keep moaning and groaning till the Day of Judgment, it will do absolutely no good. God's will happens. And after all, *we* are still very much alive. It is his own fault that he is dead now. Yes, yes, I really mean that. What in the devil was the use of it to take this morning to go to an early mass. He does that at the most only four times a year and he had to pick the day that the cathedral collapsed. They would have sung the mass just as beautifully without him hanging around. That's what the singers are paid for. It is just like my cousin

Michaut always says, 'You cannot trust death.' The very moment we think about it the least, it hits us. If we had told the dear departed yesterday, 'Dear canon, you don't have to squeeze and touch that beautiful goose we are going to eat tomorrow because you won't be invited to the meal!' he would have sworn upon his honor that no matter what happened he was going to have his share. You see, that's how easy it is to make a mistake. It is truly a pity, because the goose would successfully grace the table of a queen. Yes, yes, let us keep a happy heart. All the trouble in the world that we make for ourselves does not help us to pay a single penny of our debts. And—just between you and me—you haven't lost much. He was one who could talk girls into doing almost anything and he would promise more butter than bread. And then it would not bother his conscience at all to let the poor things wait till they were green in the face, after he had used and scolded them. And one of his greatest mistakes was that he always thought about his belly. He was drunk most of the time and owed everybody in the neighborhood money. You see, it does not even help to bring him back when I tell you the truth about him. Truly, he wasn't even worth the price of a sucked-out egg."

Madame Thomas proved to me with her eulogy for the old gentleman that our servants are but spies who make themselves judges of our morals and who are the more dangerous because they lack the power of discrimination and never see our good deeds. They are twice as malicious if they are unable to find our weaknesses and imperfections. She gave me a very long speech and everything in it was exactly the opposite from what she had to say about Brother Alexis. It is true that his way of life was such as to earn the panegyric of any female connoisseur. I just say this because I have enough imagination to fancy his ability and I have often regretted that so much talent was rendered almost inactive since it was forced to slumber under the modest rags and tatters of a mendicant monk.

# CHAPTER NINE. *BROTHER ALEXIS*

To avoid being accused that my account is rambling and not written down in proper order, let us wait till this slovenly lewd monk pay's his next visit to Madame Thomas before I tell you my story about him. But the evil is never *that* bad; let's allow him to come in while our dear landlady is turning the goose with which she is going to feed him.

You will be able to imagine that I saw a tall, erect, muscular, heavy-boned man with a full beard and a fresh, rosy complexion. His lively, penetrating eyes were fiery and their mischievous twinkle caused a tickling sensation slightly lower than my heart which could not be remedied by a thorough scratching with my fingernails. Madame Thomas told him about my sordid history. On his way to the house he had already heard about the untimely passing of our canon, but he too, like us, succeeded in quickly finding solace. The rascal did not limit his trade to collecting alms. He had discovered the secret of making himself profitably useful to society and even more so to his monastery. He serviced both sexes. No one understood better than he how to instigate tender meetings, clear away obstacles, divert the watchfulness of Argus eyes, cuckold jealous husbands, allow liberties to those young ones f whom he was supposed to take care and free fearful turtledoves from the tyrannical lordship of their fathers and mothers. In short, Alexis was the king among matchmakers and panderers and was therefore held in high esteem by gallant society.

After the first formal courtesies had been exchanged, Madame Thomas left us alone to go prepare the main course of our first meal.

She had hardly gone downstairs when Alexis kissed me heartily upon the mouth and threw me upon the bed without any further ado. Though I deemed his behavior as strange as it was unexpected, the desire I felt for him and the curiosity to see what he had hidden under his cowl made me resist just enough to fire his passions and to avoid being thought of by him as a common street whore. After he had put me down in the proper position, he raised his soutane and took out a beautiful, gorgeous tool ... an instrument which seemed more befitting to furnish the trousers of a king than the revolting and filthy fly of a poor foot soldier in the army of the Holy St. Francis. Aah, Madame Thomas, how many women would love to take thy place and buy old hats at such a price! The queen of passionate love, the adorable Cytherea herself would have gladly sacrificed both Mars and Adonis to acquire such a precious instrument. It seemed to me as if Priapus and all his followers penetrated deeply into my body. The stinging pain caused by this eternally adorable monstrosity would have made me scream out loud were it not that I feared to alarm the entire neighborhood. But this small evil was soon forgotten when I started to drown in an enormous wave of voluptuous pleasure. How could I ever describe the delicious convulsions, the intoxicating palpitations and the glorious ecstasies I underwent. Our powers of description are always too weak to depict what we feel so strongly. Is it surprising that it seems as if the very soul has been destroyed and we exist only with our senses?

I would have gladly run the risk of dying during this passionate embrace had it not been for the rough voice of Madame Thomas talking to her dog which forced us to separate. I do not believe that it was very difficult for her to guess what had transpired. Our excitement had not yet been released; our flushed faces and the rumpled bed were silent witnesses against us. But she nevertheless pretended that nothing had happened. And when the goose appeared upon the table, every one of us started to gorge himself. Between the courses of fruit and cheese, Brother Alexis took a bologna sausage and a bottle of aquavit out of his beggar's pouch, a gift from a well-meaning girl. Madame Thomas, who was a lover of these victuals, drank more than two-thirds of the bottle, which brought her into such a good mood that her eyes rolled around in her head as if she were a rutting pussy screaming for the passionate attentions of a tomcat. She was sliding up and down on her chair as if she had a bundle of thistles bound against her derriere. It seemed that the spirits of aquavit affected her that way. She jerked back and forth partly out of desire for tenderness and partly out of fury. She kissed the monk: she squeezed him; she almost licked him off; she bit him and tickled him. Finally I took pity upon the poor woman and I retired into a small side room whose walls consisted of thin boards, with cracks as wide as my fingers, that had been pasted over with thin paper. Through a small opening which I made I could watch the couple going into full action.

As the dear reader may remember, I described Madame Thomas as a heavy, contented woman who had fattened herself with her superb cooking, and therefore he should not be in the least disturbed when I tell him about the posture Brother Alexis forced her to take. The dear lady had such an enormous belly that it was absolutely impossible to enter her from the front. Even the rigs of the famous donkey stallions of *Mirebalais* in *Bretagne* could never have reached her from that position. She leaned both her elbows upon the mattress, pressed her pug nose into the pillows and presented her enormous behind to the pleasure of the venerable monk. The knave threw her skirt, underskirts and chemise way over her shoulders and unveiled the twin globes of her lower back that not only stood out because of their enormous size but also because of their snow-white color. When the angelic aspergillum, still slightly disarranged, reached the enormous cleft which it had mounted so often from below, it suddenly jumped with incredible strength through the heavy brush which obscured the inner part of said derriere and disappeared between the bushes.

During this operation Madame Thomas howled and groaned like the doomed souls in hell. This excess of passion brought her into a frenzy which normally can be caused only by terrible torture. She nevertheless succeeded in regaining her senses somewhat. "Aaah, my heavy sausage!" she hollered loudly, her voice interrupted by deep and heavy moans . . . Stop it! You are killing me ... I'm dying. Oh, my darling billy goat. . . I love you . . . You are doing it so good Come on, dear heart, gold piece of my soul! . . . Ouch, you damned son of a whore! You dog! Don't stop it now . . . you're tearing me apart! Oh, forgive me, my sweet friend . . . have pity upon me . . . I ... can ... no ... longer . . . bear ... it!

I must admit that I did not have the strength to view this passionate scene in cold blood. I was just about to use my forefinger as a rather meager substitute when I noticed a candle upon an old portable organ standing in the corner. I grabbed hold of the towering object and shoved it as deeply as I could into me without taking my eyes off the actors in front of me. Though I did not entirely extinguish the fire which consumed me, it sufficed at least to dampen my ardor a little bit and thus I acquired some release.

One should not be too surprised that Madame Thomas showed little shame during the execution of this immoral act, even though she must have known that I was in close proximity. In the first place she was in no position to think about the proper rules of behavior, and secondly even if she had been able to do so there was no reason for her to take my tender feelings into consideration since she had been fully informed about my profession. The question was whether she wanted to prove to me that she trusted me completely and wanted to become my friend or whether it was sheer debauchery and she wanted to find delight in the viewing of a similar slippery scene as she had just finished playing, but it is a fact that she pulled Brother Alexis' still steaming monstrosity out of his trousers again and pressed it into my hands. Even if I had wanted to put on a demure demeanor, I would not have had the time to do so. The lustful monk pushed me back upon the bed and made a face mask out of my skirt. His horrid, turgid firebrand which barely missed its goal gave me such a tremendous jolt against my belly that I feared it would spill my innards. The Samaritan Madame Thomas, who was witness to my torture, had the tender decency to help me. It was only because she pulled and jarred the rebellious instrument with all her power that it finally and happily disappeared into the cunthole. Since I was quite incapable of showing him my gratitude in a loud voice, my rapid pelvic movements which I performed without stopping must have left him without a doubt that I was greatly appreciative of his behavior.

The tireless friar remained unperturbed in the saddle and he reciprocated every single one of my convulsions with a rapid counterthrust. His jolts were so overpowering that on any other occasion the mere thought of it would have scared me, since I was afraid that the floorboards were about to collapse. But passion had made me lose all fear. After all, a fireplace belongs in every home and I did not have the slightest reason to be worried. This much is true: there are moments when women become truly courageous. I cannot remember that in all my born days I ever made sport with so much abandon; all I needed was a partner like Brother Alexis to remain triumphant and in control of my passions. I became a true demon. I had crossed my legs behind his knees and embraced his hips with my arms, forming such a strong vise that they would have had to hack me to pieces in order to free him. The glory of claiming victory over me was reserved for him only. What might sound incredible, yes, even unbelievable, was that he succeeded without so much as an interruption to take a deep breath in making me experience thrice in a row the delights of Mohammed's paradise. It should be a lesson to you, oh proud men of the world, that the virile outbursts of this upright man of God make your performances look tepid and can only be contributed to the miraculous virtues of the cloth!

Brother Alexis now had a very high opinion of me after he had sampled some of my talents and he assured me with the voice of a prophet that I would surely become a great success.

"It would be easy to find somebody for you who is willing to keep you," he said, "but that would not lead to anything solid or promising. You have such a beautiful face and figure that we cannot allow you to get stuck in mediocrity. If I am not mistaken, the only proper place for you is the *Opera.* I will make it my business to give you an introduction. The only question is whether you have an inclination toward singing or toward dancing."

"I believe I would have more success as a dancer," I answered.

"I believe so, too," he replied, and covered my legs up to the knees. "These limbs are created for such a task and you can take my word for it, they will keep the monocles in the *parterre* fully occupied."

# CHAPTER TEN. *THE OPERA*

Brother Alexis was not a man of false promises. He immediately proceeded to write a letter of introduction to a certain Monsieur de Gr . . M . . ., who was at that time the leaseholder of all the charms of the girls at the *Theatre Lyrique.* The next morning Madame Thomas loaned me the necessary odds and ends; I dressed myself up as carefully as I could and before the afternoon I carried the letter to his address.

In front of me stood a tall, thin man with a leathery face whose phlegmatic expression exuded a coolness that went through bone and marrow. He wore a flattering morning robe but no trousers. A slight breeze played with his shirt and showed now and then two strong, cadaverous, bony thighs between which the limp relics of his manhood dangled downwards.

I noticed how his eyes occasionally glanced over me carefully while he was reading the letter and how his stern face gradually brightened. I took this for a good omen as far as my opportunities were concerned and I was not mistaken. Monsieur de Gr. . . M. . . invited me to sit next to him and mentioned that a girl as pretty and well-built as I was had no need for an introduction. But he would seize the opportunity to render a service to the public by presenting a find like me. While he was praising me with so many beautiful words he was also taking a thorough inventory of my most secret charms. And since the spirit of wickedness awakened his lechery step by step, the whoremaster pressed his lamentable flacidity into my hands. Now my time had come to employ all the knowledge I had gathered in Madame Florence's house at such a great expense, to see if I was up to the task of reviving this formless mass. Since it seemed to be totally impervious and insensitive to my rubbing and pulling, and even the squeezing of the testicles bore no results, I started to doubt if my efforts would ever become successful. I had almost given up when the idea hit me to tickle his anus and sodomize him with my fingertip. The unconscious engine suddenly jumped up out of its lethargy and developed such a remarkable manner that it seemed almost to become an entirely different being. To fully employ this precious moment and to crown my most important job, I moved my closed hand so enticingly yet firmly up and down that the monster was overpowered by the sweetest sensations and ejected big tears of gratitude which I kissed away.

Finally Monsieur de Gr . . . M . . ., who was ecstatic about the method I had employed, dressed hastily and personally took me over to see Monsieur Thuret who was at that time the director of the *Opera.* I was very happy that this gentleman liked me at first sight. Without thinking twice he allowed me to join the ranks of the charming young ladies of the *Academie de musique royale* and also invited us to dinner.

Since I prefer to bring variation into my recountings and descriptions, I will not bore you with an account of what happened that evening between Monsieur Thuret and me. Suffice it to say that the man was as horny a goat as Monsieur de Gr . . . M . . ., and it was just as difficult to get him into action.

I went back to Madame Thomas' to go to sleep but she was still awake and impatiently burning with the desire to find out everything that had transpired from Brother Alexis' letter. The next morning I moved into my new home, where I did not have to be afraid of police interference any longer.

Aside from the training in the storehouse, where I never failed to show up, I also received private lessons from "Malther the Devil." I progressed so rapidly that within three months I was able to stay reasonably on my toes during the ballet.

The day of my first performance was marked by a rather funny interlude. One of my colleagues had been caught in the theater while committing a deadly sin. The female part of the conclave barely had time to digest this tidbit of news when they clamored for a severe punishment to give all of us a frightening example. The delinquent appeared before the tribunal of Monsieur Thuret to hear the verdict. The supervisor, *La Chamaree,* was willing to show mercy. But Madame Cartou, who was closely watched by her fellow-jurors, the ladies Fanchon-Chopine, Desaigles and Mother Superior Carville, declared that the consequences could be very dangerous if such missteps were forgiven; novices could be encouraged by lack of punishment to commit monstrous excesses, and might even cause a revolt among the girls of the *Opera comique.* She added that it was unforgivable and dishonorable to allow such indecencies to happen in this theater which, ever since its foundation, had been a model for the most tender and charming gallantry and courtesy. They had to punish this criminal female severely or else it would not take long ere no decent girl would be willing to join the ranks at the *Opera.* Madame Fanchon-Chopine gave her final opinion and insisted that the girl should be immediately stricken off the payroll. Monsieur Thuret, who was very well aware of the fact that he could do nothing to change the minds of those blockheads, declared that the guilty girl had lost all honor and privileges and was immediately, without the right of protest, released from the opportunity to show her pretty face and beautiful legs ever again upon the stage of this august institution.

# CHAPTER ELEVEN. *MY FINANCIER*

My ballet shoes had already twirled for more than two weeks among the pupils of Terpsichore, when I found the following letter upon awakening one beautiful morning. It read as follows:

*Mademoiselle:*

*I noticed you yesterday in the Opera. I like your face. When you feel the desire to reach an agreement with a man who is horrified at the thought of objections during amorous dalliance and who never utters a sigh of love with an empty pocket, please be so kind as to let me know your reply by return. I remain . . .*

Even though I had very little experience with society and did not possess the knowledge to classify people by their writing style, I instinctively presumed from the blunt and short language of this note that I had touched the heart of a financier. Acquaintanceships of this calibre are too precious to ignore when they show up. So I decided not to pretend to be a prude and wrote an immediate answer. I told him I felt greatly honored that he preferred me above the many other most charming young ladies he had seen at the *Opera*. And it would be very bad manners if I did not recompense his kindness and accept his dear invitation. And since he was waiting so impatiently to meet me, I assured him that the pleasure was entirely mine.

He appeared an hour after my answer in a beautifully appointed *equipage* which, without being ostentatious, showed the wealth of its owner. I met him, properly veiled. To paint his picture in a few words: he was a little, thickset and terribly ugly man of around sixty. When he entered, a few gallant phrases bubbled from his lips and I would not have understood a single word were it not for the fact that he discreetly slipped a roll of fifty *louis d'or* into my hands. There are absolutely no unfriendly greetings when they are accompanied by such a noble gesture; every word becomes admirable and heartening. It was not only what he said to me that seemed so friendly and artistically expressed but I also seemed to discover traits of nobility and refined manners in his features which might have escaped me at first glance. That happens to be the result of good manners: one can always be sure of being well-liked when one knows how to behave upon entering another's home.

I wore my most charming, passion-evoking *deshabille.* The artfulness which I had employed so closely resembled nature itself that my charms did not seem to need any help from costume or cosmetics. The effect was precisely as I had expected. My financier thought me adorable. His passionate glances and the impatience of his hands left no doubt that I would not remain untouched. But what happened? After fumbling around for almost an hour, I experienced the most horrendous failure. This humiliating adventure pained me deeply, especially since this was the first time that such a thing had ever happened to me. I shuddered at the thought that he might have discovered some imperfection of which I had hitherto been totally unaware. But fortunately I recovered my courage when he confessed to me that such incidents quite frequently happened to him. In fact, the good man spoke the truth. During the entire year in which I lived together with him, he failed with the regularity of a timepiece twice a week. And even though this was a terrible fact, many a girl would have been very happy if she had been in my place under similar circumstances. He had decorated and furnished a home for me in the *rue Sainte-Anne,* paid for the entire cost of my household and gave me every month one hundred *pistoles.* I had a beautiful opportunity to make a fortune out of this acquaintanceship when he suddenly lost his. This unexpected event interrupted not only my means of income but also our love life. At the *Opera* everything depends upon the acquisition of a certain fame. Nothing brings an actress more acclaim than the reputation of having been the cause of several bankruptcies and having utterly ruined several of her admirers. The downfall of my financier brought me an incredible fame. A whole band of new admirers from all ranks begged to be introduced to me. But I did not want to make a decision without getting the good advice of Monsieur de Gr . . . M . . . and of Brother Alexis. I felt deeply indebted to both gentlemen. I will include here, in parentheses, so to speak, the wholesome advice I received from them, as a sort of monument of my gratitude and as a dependable guide for every girl who wants to make a good profit from her charms.

### ADVICE FOR A PRETTY GIRL

*Every girl or woman who wants to make her fortune in this world has to keep in mind, constantly, only her own interest and her own gain, just like any other merchant.

*Her heart should be closed to love at all times. It is sufficient if she pretends to experience love and knows how to make others fall for her.

*Whosoever pays the most must have preference over all other rivals. At least she should make a comparison between him and people of standing because the majority of them are arrogant and thievish. The great, persistent financiers are more solid and easier to dominate. One must know how to take them.

*If she is smart, she will rid herself of every paramour unless his upkeep does not cost her a penny. It often happens that he drives away those upon whom her livelihood depends. If she nevertheless wants to keep a paramour to pass her idle time in amorous exploits, she should never feel pangs of conscience, because these little affairs are the incidentals which may keep her happy.

*She should imitate to the best of her ability the frugality of *Mademoiselle Durocher,* the mistress of Lord

Weymouth, and only enjoy the delicious morsels when they don't cost her Lord and Master any money.

*She should invest her money carefully and get the best interest from it.

*When she likes a foreigner and a Frenchman equally well and both compete for her favors, she should not hesitate to select the former. Entirely aside from the dictates of good manners, she will greatly enhance her fortune, especially if she can enter into affairs with the Mylords from the City of London. These people, though basically poor suckers, are capable of ruining themselves financially out of pride, just so they can be considered richer than we are.

*She will do very well, especially, to protect her health, in avoiding any contact with Americans, Spaniards and Neapolitans; and let herself be guided by the rule: *Timeo Danaos Et Dona Ferentes'*

*One final warning: she should never express her own opinions. She should carefully study the individuality of her lover and disguise herself with it as if it were her own.

sig. Gr . . . M . . . and Fr. Alexis, OFM.

I do hope that all the girls of my profession will imprint this codex deeply into their memories, and that they make good use of it, as I did!

# CHAPTER TWELVE. *THE BARON*

The first one who fell into my snares to replace the old financier was a baron, the son of a German wholesale merchant from the city of Hamburg. I do not believe that there was ever a more stupid and disagreeable creature to come out of Germany. He was as tall as a beanpole, bow-legged, a flaming redhead, a high-grade ass and an incurable alcoholic to boot. This 'cavalier,' the hope and idol of his family, traveled around Europe to round out the talents with which Nature had blessed him through contact with those that are commonly referred to as the fairer sex. The only decent house he knew in Paris was that of his banker who had been ordered to pay him as much as he wanted. His only company consisted of two or three spongers who told him whatever they expected he would like, and a few cheap bunnies he had picked up from Madame Lacroix' seraglio.

Monsieur de Gr . . . M . . ., who was as much devoted to my interests as his own, was of the opinion that it would be a pity if this pigeon could not be locked up in our cage. He insinuated to the baron that it was almost indecent when a nobleman like himself did not live up to the expectations which his high station in life required of him. Nothing was more *en vogue* and modern for the man of distinction, and nothing could do more to enhance his honor than to keep a *demoiselle* from the theater. In a word, it was precisely through such liaisons that our young gentlemen from the better classes and the jurists of any standing acquired their gallant manners and were accepted as *bon ton* in high society.

The baron was highly pleased with this sensible advice and confessed that he had longed for a love affair with a girl from the *Opera* and that he would consider himself extremely lucky if I could be the one.

"I'll be blasted!" exclaimed Monsieur de Gr ... M—
"That is what I call a true display of extremely good taste.
It is as if you had lived in Paris for more than ten years! Do
you realize that from time immemorial there has not been
such an incredibly charming creature ever to grace the
stages of Paris? She has been unencumbered for the past
month and she cannot make up her mind to whom she will
allow the honor to protect her. The poor child is literally
besieged with offers. I will take it upon myself to handle
your best interests. Between you and me, the only hope I
can give you is that I happen to know she has a weakness
for those foreign devils. But I also want you to understand
that she is not very interested in material things. She is the
kind of girl that could easily fall in love with you, provided
your behavior toward her is utterly correct. You would not
believe me if I told you how much she was devoted to her
former lover. And they deserved each other. Nobody has
ever seen a nobler and more unselfish couple. She tried in
vain to keep her needs secret from him—you must undoubtedly understand that a young and charming lady is invariably in need of a few odds and ends ... But he possessed the
most amazing discernment and would always find out about
it. And then, whenever he paid for it those two would have
the most touching quarrels, setting an example for all the
world in magnanimity and generosity."

The baron, who was pleasantly surprised with the
laudable commendation about me, begged Monsieur de Gr
... M ... to bring about an introduction to me as quickly as
he possibly could and told him not to regard any cost as an
obstacle.

Fully intending to heighten his ardor, I decided not
to be in a hurry and let a couple of days pass ere I would
notify him of my decision. We finally met for the first time
at the *Opera* during a repeat performance of "Jephta,"
where he was greatly honored to be allowed backstage to

kiss my hand respectfully. I was not too annoyed that he met me during a repeat performance, because it is on those occasions that the ladies show up in all their splendor, surrounded by the glitter and dignity of their positions, trying their best to make each other jealous by showing off the spendthrift and humiliating foibles of their scatterbrained lovers.

Even though I had only brought one single man to ruination, I already owned a considerable amount of jewelry and many valuable trifles, and was seated among the most important mistresses, which meant that I had my own chair at the side of the orchestra. I had crossed my legs rather carelessly. It was very cold but unfortunately it was customary to be seen in valuable and impressive *negliges.* Draped in ermine, mink and sable, I kept my feet in a box which was covered with crimson-colored silk and lined with bearskin while its temperature was raised by periodically changing tin bulbs filled with boiling water. In this proud getup I whittled away with a small golden weaver's shuttle, and with a bored expression I looked now and then at my watch and let it ring. I opened and closed all my snuff boxes, one after another, and whisked from time to time a valuable rock-crystal flask under my nose to cure myself of the vapors I did not have. I bent over to say nothing to my colleague in order to give the curious monocles a chance to judge the elegant bearing of my limbs. In short, I committed thousands of naughty and impudent little acts which delighted the simpletons among the audience. Whenever my eyes met someone, who thereupon deeply and respectfully bowed, I could be sure to make him delirious with happiness if I deigned to return his greeting with a hardly recognizable nod.

At this moment of triumph it was very, very difficult for me to remember my first position of employment. The luxury which surrounded me, the obeisance of those who paid me court, had wiped out all of these memories. I believed myself to be a goddess. And how could I have thought otherwise when I was surrounded by the blind adoration and the tokens of precious admiration of the highest ranking personages? Let us be honest about this: it is the men and not we who should be accused of our carefree and spendthrift behavior. Because it is they who distort our sense of values and turn our heads with their miserable submission, their flattery and their inanities. Why shouldn't we indulge, since they give us their example and forget their dignity completely? I cannot help but admit this shame for both parties involved. Our only merit exists mainly in the lecherous fantasies and the perverted tastes of our admirers. Excuse me, my dear girls, for the frankness I have used in this little reprimand. My open-heartedness will not harm your interests and it is far from me to wish such a thing. And as long as there are men in this world, you will never have trouble finding one who will be willingly led by the nose.

But let us return to our baron. I had noticed with much pleasure that my slight attentive-ness toward him had thrown him into the frenzies of ecstatic delight; he had lost his freedom. From the beginning to the end of the performance his eyes were glued to me like a dog on a leash and he seemed to thrive on the contemplation of my many charms. After the performance I allowed him to invite me into his coach, and did him the honor of having supper with him. Monsieur de Gr . . . M ..., who had remained in the theater because of some sort of unfinished business, joined us about a quarter of an hour later. Since I did not want to destroy the glorious picture that he had painted of me to the baron, I remained very reticent throughout the entire evening and I played my act so naturally, pretending to be a tender young maiden, that the poor idiot in all seriousness believed I was capable of such feelings.

Nature has the habit of equalizing the injustice she has wrought in stupid people with a considerable dose of egotism. The more blunt and unsympathetic they are, the more firmly they believe that they are a boon to society. And this was also the weakness of my hero. He did not doubt for one moment that I was as smitten with his charms as he was with mine. And it was a very heavy task for me to make this flattering impression seem true to him. During supper I was a veritable picture of good graces and shy humility. And when he retired, my looks told him that I loved him—he would have sworn upon that—and that I expected him tomorrow between ten and eleven o'clock to drink chocolate with me. (That was the time I had intended to find out exactly how generous he would be.) His arrival was so punctual that I was still in bed when he was announced. I quickly put on my morning robe, and since I did not have to be afraid, like most girls, of being seen in my natural state without having to employ all the tricks of artful make-up and tedious toiletry, I received him in a very simple *neglige;* however, with all the little hypocrisies and commonplaces which are expected on such occasions.

"Oh, but my dear baron, is that really nice to surprise people so unexpectedly? But my dear God, what time is it? Your watch must be fast, it could not possibly be eleven o'clock. Oh, dear Lord have pity upon me. It is all my fault. Oh, I really hate myself for this. I am terrible . . . awful, am I not? Oh, you may as well admit it. Oh, how awful that you have to catch me red-handed with my untidiness. But I want you to know that I have not slept a wink since last night. Right now, this very moment, I have the most terrible migraine; it is driving me to distraction. But it does not matter, the joy to see you again will surely make it go away. Come, Lisette, be quick. Serve the chocolate. And don't forget, I don't want it too thin."

My orders were carried out quickly. And while our noses inhaled the sweet aroma which permeated the entire mansion, and we sipped from the delicious, frothy liquid, I was told that my jeweler wanted to see me.

"What? Why, these terrible interruptions!" I exclaimed. "Don't you know that I am not at home to anybody? Oh, these servants, it makes absolutely no difference to them what the instructions are, they always want it their own way. It makes me furious . . . But, if you don't mind, my dear baron, now I *am* really curious to find out what he wants. Lisette, show the gentleman in ... Ah, good morning, my dearest Monsieur de la Frenaye! If I may ask, what brings you here so early in the day? How is your business? I make a bet that you have something you want to show me."

"Madame," he answered, "allow me to interrupt you. Since I happened to be in the neighborhood, I took the liberty to presume that you might want to see this beautiful cross which was ordered by the wife of a banker from the *Place Vendome*. And without wanting to be presumptuous, I may say that it is one of the most delicate and precious pieces of jewelry that has ever been made."

"You are really very courteous, Monsieur de la Frenaye, not to forget your friends. I really appreciate this token of your attentiveness. So allow me to have a look at it, since you seem to be so proud of it ... Oh, Baron, look how beautiful! This setting is simply gorgeous. I have hardly ever seen such a beautiful piece of jewelry. Look at those stones, aren't they cut with a perfect brilliance? Don't you think that their sparkle is almost magical? Those impudent banker's wives nowadays wear such a beautiful thing and display a grandeur which is neither becoming nor fitting for them. To be very frank with you, I think it is a shame that a woman of that kind should own such a splendid jewel... Please, do tell me, how much is it worth?"

"Madame," answered de la Frenaye, "it is 8,000 francs and that is as low as I can go."

"If I had the money," I went on, "I simply could not stand the idea that you were to take it out of my house again."

"But you know, Madame, that everything I have can be yours at your beck and call. For less than you believe . . ."

"No! Absolutely not. It is not my habit to buy on credit."

The baron, who, as I had anticipated, was delighted to find such a beautiful opportunity to pay me court, took the cross, paid the jeweler immediately 60 *louis d'or* in cash and wrote a promise to pay the remainder the next day. I played the part of the girl who is upset because she is modest and unselfish, up to the hilt.

"Now, really, dear Baron, that is the height of absurdity! That is truly overstepping the boundaries of generosity. I will be very frank with you. You did not give me any pleasure with such a gesture. I believe there is nothing wrong with accepting some small knick-knacks from somebody one likes and to whom a girl is dearly attracted; but, honestly . . . this is too much! I really cannot make up my mind whether I should accept this."

While I said these things, the dunce hung the cross around my neck, whereupon I went into my bedroom, deeply in thought. He followed me. And without making him drool too long, I allowed him to cash in on my gratitude at the foot of my bed for the 8,000 francs he had just spent; without losing the illusion of my natural tenderness so that the blockhead firmly believed I liked him for his good characteristics and my attraction for his person rather than for the beautiful gift I had so cunningly wheedled out of him.

I had informed Monsieur de Gr . . . M . . . the previous night about my intentions to give the purse of my noble suitor a thorough bloodletting, and he did not fail to show up that afternoon to accept a gift of a beautiful golden snuff box a *la Maubois* as his broker's fee. Since he did not have to go to the *Opera* that night, we had dinner together. And both of us had good reason to be very satisfied with our finished business. Cheer was the main course of our dinner. The baron was in such a good mood that he kept paying us his Germanic compliments in the most monstrously mangled language. But the constant wetting of his throat took away the last remnants of what little sound mind he had and we finally had to send him on his way, drunk as a Lord, to his own home.

After this successful test of his generosity, I thought that I would do much better if I did not attach myself to him completely but kept up my role of the passionate woman carrying a torch. This behavior of mine was far more successful than I had dared dream. The month had hardly passed ere I was in possession of a complete service, including all the flatware. Even though it will always remain true that foreign generosities cause hostility rather than gratitude, the friendly act I had to perform almost daily nearly caused me to seriously fall in love with the baron. Habit breeds intimacy, if I may paraphrase, and one becomes accustomed to the slight faults of people who are our daily acquaintances. Even though my German baron was terribly foul-mouthed and stupid, I deemed him gradually less unsympathetic. But, suddenly, a terrible impropriety he committed made him irrevocably repulsive to me.

As I have mentioned before, he was in the habit of drinking quite a lot. And unfortunately he felt himself more attracted to me whenever he was in that condition. So after we had spent one day in a rather uncommunicative manner and I had decided to go to bed after dinner, the stupid glutton stumbled over the door step, lost his equilibrium and fell flat on his face on my parquet floor. In his condition that tumble could not have been harmless and when they tried to lift him up, he did not move and his face was covered with blood. If I had had the opportunity to faint, I would not have hesitated to do so. But he needed help badly so I decided instead to run into my dressing room, and I returned with three or four bottles.

Since I believed the damage to be more serious than it was in reality, I was not just satisfied with washing his face and rinsing his mouth. I also wanted to administer a teaspoonful of wonderwater. But the dirty bum had barely tasted a few drops of it ere he started to heave, and threw up three quarters of his dinner right in my face. I could try in vain, since I would not be able to describe this disgusting scene, so let it suffice to say that I almost heaved blood, that I had to change gowns and almost used four *louis d'or* worth of perfumes and creams to cleanse myself. I was so furious that I had him thrown out of my home and gave his manservant the message that he could tell his Master never to set foot in my house again.

When the baron, upon awakening the next morning, found out what had happened and received the message I had given him, he nearly went out of his mind. He wrote me several letters but I refused to accept them. Finally he realized that a visit to Monsieur de Gr . . . M . . . was his last resort. And by doing so, our pigeon had delivered himself into the talons of a hawk. That shrewd panderer did not dream of alleviating the baron's fears. Instead, he accused him of criminal behavior and decided that there was simply not one single ground for attaining my forgiveness. The poor, utterly devastated baron cried, howled, groaned and made such a complete fool of himself that Monsieur de Gr . . . M . . . began to fear that the man would be dumb enough to hang himself, in which case we would have been left holding the bag. He therefore deemed it wiser to change his pitch.

"You have an affair with the nicest, kindest most forgiving girl in the world," he told the baron, "and that may be the saving grace in your case. Even though the insult you committed toward her is almost unbelievable, I have no doubt that your true penitence and humility will not fail to soften her heart sooner or later. I have good reason to believe this, because I happen to know that she is hopelessly in love with you and that the certain pride with which she arms herself is merely because she deems it improper to show you her true feelings. Nevertheless, she always fails completely in keeping up her guard all the time, and in those instances she invariably decides in your favor. Why, just yesterday ... no, no, let me finish . . . Yesterday, I said, she was unable to keep back her tears when I happened to mention your name. She even confessed to me that she had never met anybody, no matter who it might have been, who had caused her to love so tenderly as you did. You can be assured: the poor child has not slept more than four hours altogether since you two had your little quarrel. And do you really want to know how much bad luck she is suffering? While she is about to collapse under the burden of her grief—which *you* caused her to suffer—some asinine decorator wants to sell her furniture for a pittance because she owes him two thousand *thaler.*"

"Vivat!" exclaimed the baron while he embraced him. "Without realizing it, you have just offered me the most wonderful opportunity to make my peace with her. I insist upon taking over her debts. Tomorrow morning I will pay that scoundrel, or he will find himself without any more clients in all of Paris."

"I'll be . . ." retorted Monsieur de Gr . . . M ... "That is a marvelous thought. Though the idea is so simple, it wouldn't have occurred to me in a hundred years! But it is truly worthy of a noble gentleman like yourself and a boon to the darling creature that inspired you to it. Yes I fully agree with you. It is well nigh impossible to think of a better way to conquer her grudge against you. She is far too tenderhearted not to be touched to the very depths of her sweet soul by the nobility of such a generous gesture. I would advise you to get the money as quickly as possible and return to me immediately. I will take care of the rest."

Well, the sacrificial lamb was in so much of a hurry that de Gr . . . M . . . brought him to me the very next day, carrying two hundred and fifty beautiful new *louis d'or.* At the melodious sound of these gold coins a river of tears sprang up in my eyes and the whole situation became so melodramatic that the baron bleated like a sheep. Our reconciliation was so touching that I almost fainted because of a laughing fit.

One has to be as phlegmatic as de Gr . . . M ... to watch a ridiculous scene like that with a stone face. After the heart-rending manner in which we made up for our little disagreement, the love and generosity of the baron became so great that I could have taken him for all he was worth had it not been for his upright father who had been informed from time to time about the most unusual invoices his dear son was paying. And one day this man arrived from Paris to personally tear the refugee Adonis from Hamburg out of my embraces.

# CHAPTER THIRTEEN. *THE CAVALIER*

Because of the enormous contribution I had managed to wrangle out of enemy territory, I had decided to be maintained exclusively by foreigners and thus increase my fortune rapidly, since I had absolutely no desire to grow old in my trade. According to my calculations I should be able to find three or four more blockheads like the last one who could feather my nest for the remainder of my career. But that case had been an exception and he was not that easily replaced.

To avoid idleness, I decided to make some raids among my compatriots and try to find a fitting replacement for my baron.

It was an established custom among the *mattresses* to frequent those places where society usually gathered. It meant that we had said our farewells to our keepers and implied that both our hearts and homes were vacant and for rent. Following this time-honored and profitable custom, I showed up at those places that were most frequented, except at *les Tuileries* which we avoided ever since the painful experience of *Mademoiselle Durocher.*

The *Palais Royal* was a territory as suitable and proper, and by hallowed tradition just as fitting as the *Opera,* which meant that we were completely free in these public gardens to be-have like proper ladies and allow the passersby full view of our charms, our artful make-up and our voluptuous gowns, without fear of retaliation. In vain, certain mocking critics were shameless enough to say that the royal palace and its gardens were the ideal places to meet profiteers, pimps and prostitutes. Their vile and dark intimations did not deter, however, the beautiful, idle youth of Paris, the chic gentry the lawyers and the men of the cloth, from getting together daily at those places, especially in the evenings before and after the theater. A large number of charming ladies of every conceivable variety formed the main decoration. The lines that were formed upon the benches under the large trees of the promenade made many a head turn. They offered the onlooker a festive, pleasing and relaxing view while the variety was truly astonishing, and the multitude defied description. Thousands of little girls huddled together like sparrows on a tree branch exuding an aroma of lascivious-ness. There is no other place in the world like it. But what could possibly be so remarkable about it? If it is true that we are the soul of all pleasures, if it is correct and proper to chase us, then why shouldn't our gathering places be the most beautiful ones in the world? The secret gift, which enables us to enchant and cheer up any gentleman who selects our company, is indeed so inseparable from our personalities that voluptuousness and debauchery follow us even into the Holy of Holies. The best proof of that is the Church of the Hospital for the Blind. It was our privilege to carry on in that place just as shamelessly as around the *Palais Royal* and our *Opera*. During the services we would be pursued with promising gestures, artful obeisances or the loud clicking of the handles of *lorgnettes*. They even go much further than that: they lean forward and whisper suggestive jokes into our ears. Our replies are equally as kind and charming, our suggestions just as daring, frequently interrupted by laughter and giggles which we try to hide by holding our fans in front of our faces. Meanwhile the Mass draws to an end while we have not had a chance to watch the motions of the priest; yes, sometimes we are not even aware whether he is standing in front of the altar or not. Our pious devotions usually result in a small supper at one of the *petites maisons,* or in a little intrigue.

One day, I agreed to an affair which disappointed me most painfully. One of those most charming lady's escorts, who are so adept at embezzling, who, thanks to the unpardonable carelessness of the chief of police, prowl around in Paris and show off their splendor, and create uproars at the expense of the same decent people they fleece, one of those depraved rascals, I said, whose pompous manners impress everybody, had discovered the secret of how to participate in every entertainment. Whether it was a trip into the *Bois de Boulogne,* or a supper, one would have died of boredom if Monsieur le Chevalier had not been present.

I had accidentally observed that an affair with this despicable breed is the more dangerous since most of them have a sweet and ingratiating character which allows them to combine an indulging and easy-going temper with the most courtly and obliging manners. To make it brief, they possess to a great extent that which is improperly considered perfect manners in polite society. I must add that this experience has taught me to beware of personages with impeccable manners and extravagant courtliness, because people like that are very seldom honorable and trustworthy.

Let me tell you about this fortune hunter. For a long time now, I had coveted the gorgeous diamond ring on his finger. The chiseler had quite frequently hinted that he deemed it too slight a payment for even the smallest of my attentions. Even though I pretended that I did not trust him, I had too high an opinion of my own charms to believe that he was merely joking. I therefore did not doubt in the least that this beautiful ring would sooner or later be mine. I was only waiting for the proper opportunity to strip him of his possession. One fine Sunday morning, during Mass in the Hospital of the Blind, I thought I finally had my chance. My cavalier found a place next to me and after he had started a gallant conversation, spiked with all sorts of sweet nothings, I answered that I considered his flattering talk very delightful if I could only be convinced that it came from his heart.

"Ah!" he exclaimed with a deep sigh, "do your eyes only have the capacity to discover great possibilities in others, and are they closed to your own great qualities?"

"Let us assume that I have any," I countered, "would that give me less reason to mistrust the palaver of gentlemen? Is that not precisely the way you daily flatter women into submission, women that are far worthier than I am? Oh, Monsieur le Chevalier, if I were to put you on the spot and desire a token of your sincerity, I am sure it would greatly embarrass you!"

"What?" he exclaimed. "Do you believe I am capable of double-dealing . . .?"

"I believe you," I interrupted him, "as much as I do all the others who half of the time say what they don't mean and often make promises which they have not the slightest intention of keeping. For instance—yes, yes, and I am not joking now—you must admit that you would be greatly embarrassed if I were to take you up on your promise when you offered me your diamond."

"Madame," he answered in a deeply hurt tone of voice. "Ere you make up your mind about people in such a derogatory manner, I think it would be only fair if you were to put me to the test."

"What do you expect?" I said smilingly. "The good ones must suffer for the deeds of the bad ones. In general, men are so deceitful that I do not consider it an injustice when we girls do not have a better opinion of your ilk. But since I do not really have any true reason which forces me to pass judgment upon you personally, I am more than willing to make an exception in your favor and assume that you have none of the bad qualities of your sex but only those which make it so desirable. But I do not think that this is the proper place to go any further into such speculations. Why don't you come with me and have a small cup of soup during which we can continue this metaphysical discussion to our heart's content."

That was exactly what this cheat had hoped I would do. The first thing he did when we entered my home, was to put the ring on my finger. The rapture into which the possession of this precious jewel brought me, made it impossible for me not to give in to any and all of his wishes and desires. Before and after dinner I gave him as many tokens of my gratitude as he wanted. But do you think I had gained anything out of this affair? The diamond was a fake. I discovered that one of my most valuable gold snuff boxes was missing; the scoundrel had absconded with it. My only real gain consisted of one of those infirmities which the doctors at *Saint-Come* generally treat with cooling diuretics and blood cleansing potions. And the worst thing of this whole miserable adventure was that I did not dare to take vengeance or to complain about the infamous behavior of this swindler. I was far more afraid that *he* would talk, and I believe that I would have paid *him* for keeping the whole sordid affair a secret. But I was smart enough to patiently swallow my pride and to go on the prescribed diet without crying over spilled milk. And to make sure that I would derive the greatest benefit from my medicine, I pretended to suffer from chest pains so that Monsieur Thuret allowed me a leave of absence from my dancing chores. Of course, I still sought out the *Opera,* but I pretended that I wished to remain incognito and seated myself in the amphitheater, now and then glancing at the stage with a bored expression on my face. My good Lord, the number of absurdities with which I enriched the audience by answering all the stupid and boring proposals and suggestions is simply staggering! From the left and from the right, a whole flock of chatterers, whispering every single absurdity into my ears! Is it really possible that men are so frivolous, and do they have to go into such detailed descriptions? And is it truly possible that we hanker after these superficial flatteries and lowly compliments, and do we enjoy listening to these inanities so much that we are the cause of them being uttered in the first place?

# CHAPTER FOURTEEN. *THE ABBE*

Among the enormous number of lamebrains was a banker with a rather blemished complexion, but of a tall build, who whispered with incredible daring the most unspeakable obscenities into my ears. These stupidities could only be the inventions of a demented mind. And an old, toothless commander—a real flatterer who would be capable of making even the most boring people fall asleep—tried his best to make me fall for his reddish, charming little slit-eyes by repeating an uncounted number of lines and phrases from the *Roman d'Astree.* Seated at some distance from these two champion roosters was a younger generation of idiots who threw passionate glances in my direction and whispered so softly to one another that their carefully phrased compliments made me dizzy. I was enchanting, a divine beauty, I surpassed the angels and my glitter was more brilliant than the stars. And whenever I looked in their direction, they glanced demurely at their fingertips to convince me of the sincerity of their remarks concerning my charms and to make sure that I would understand they were not meant to be overheard by me.

And the more I thought about so much impudence, the more I was tempted to believe that either creatures like us had an incredible magnetic influence or that men had to be utterly blind beings. But, however this may be, the ridiculous desire, which is rampant throughout France, to have an affair with a girl from the theater rather than with the women of the kingdom who fully deserve male attention by right of birth or merit, is widespread and has become a symbol of status. Is it possible that such shortsightedness can be ascribed to mere vanity, to the ridiculous desire to be talked about? It really seems to me that our existence gives substance to the lives of our lovers. Even though many of them do not distinguish themselves from the masses, even if they bring themselves to ruin—the moment they let themselves in with one of us, they can no longer be ignored. They have become men *a la mode*. How many despicable leaseholders would have gone through life completely unnoticed if they had not taken part in our piracies and embezzlements. It is we that pull these people out of their obscurity and give them a halo of fame, and who consecrate their names with the incredible amounts of money we make them spend on us. Is not the fame of *Duliz* entirely due to *Mademoiselle Pelissier?* And it is without doubt this incomparable siren who has enriched our courtly status with the history of this famous Israelite. Thanks to the number of diamonds she swindled out of him and thanks to all the adventures which were a direct result of this, his memory will live on throughout eternity. It is not only enough to know that such an incredibly wealthy man really existed, it is far better to have the knowledge that the wretched devil, so to speak, died in the poorhouse on a straw bed. This is the fabulous fame one can acquire: utter ruination through frequently visiting us. Of course, it has its compensations—public renown and the inner delight of having created a stir in respectable society. But, let us return to my own story.

For more than three weeks I had tried to refresh my blood with a brew made out of strawberry roots, sea urchins and saltpeter, when my milliner advised me that I could make use of the services of a member of the ecclesiastical authorities. Even though I felt hale and hearty at that time, I was not yet convinced of having been fully cured and I was still in doubt whether my rosebush could be approached without the danger of being stung by a possible thorn.

If it had been a member of the laity with whom I had been required to enter into an affair, it would not have bothered my conscience one whit to leave it up to fate and have him run the risk of regretting our get-together. But since it concerned a priest, my only concern was to clean him out thoroughly without laying myself open to the possibility of the occurrence of any incidents. Because it takes a thief to catch a thief.

Since it is these gentlemen's profession to impress people in everything, using the hypocritical veil of Christian and moral virtues, moreover, since these devout papists are willing to preach to us for one single franc those matters which they would not do themselves for a hundred-thousand, in a word, since the swindlers of this world do not offer their services with any other goal in mind than to fatten themselves upon the fruits of hard labor and then derisively laugh about our tremendous expenses, I firmly believed I would render a service rather than commit a crime if I accidentally were to give such a person a reason and an opportunity to complain about my behavior. Therefore, after careful consideration, I decided to be willing and ready to receive his attentions. I had also firmly made up my mind to relieve him—if at all possible—of everything, including his last clerical collar.

Just imagine some kind of a satyr, as shaggy as Lycaon, whose puffy and haggard looks betrayed a sensual temperament and a failing will to abstinence which was clearly shown in his features, where sheer lust shone through his hypocritically veiled gaze . . . But, let us not finish his portrait because I am afraid that my quill would not do him justice and a malicious reader might draw the wrong conclusions. I never had expected from a man of the cloth the gallantry he showed me. It was as graceful and elegant as one of those repeater watches made by *Julien le Roi,* full of incredibly intertwined dainty and decorative ornaments, sprinkled here and there with pearls and diamonds. I must admit, upon my word of honor, that I had never seen a member of the clergy who was a better example of the exception to the famous rule, "Every good priest is a poor man." On the contrary, he was such a stupid spendthrift that it did not take me more than two weeks before he had to start selling his indulgences for one thousand *louis a* piece. He was just the man who would have sold out the entire clergy just to please me, if I had not given him the message that I was ill and indisposed. When the truth sank in, his love for me turned into blind fury and it would not have taken much more to push him over the brink and have him commit an assault upon me. I therefore sought refuge in the brazen boldness to which the women of my profession are so well-versed. I talked to him so firmly that he was thunderstruck. I told him in no uncertain terms that I considered it a hazardous undertaking to insult me in such a shameless manner. It would do him justice if I had him thrown out of my window. The only thing he could possibly accuse me of, was my weakness for him. I moreover added that I had found out—to my utter surprise—how true the rumors were about people of his rank and standing; that I now had found out for myself how fully they deserved their horrible reputation of debauchees and libertines. I held that he might conceivably be used to that certain breed of women which dwells in houses of ill-repute. I also mentioned that, if it were not for that little bit of pity I still had for his unfortunate person, I would not hesitate to call in the authorities and have him arrested on the spot. And I made it plain that I had enough influence in certain circles to have him put away in a place where he could spend the remainder of his days in penance and chastisement to correct the vile ways in which he was wasting his earthly life.

This short and severe preaching had the effect I desired. The stricken spreader of the Gospel was so flabbergasted and so humiliated that he disappeared without uttering another sound. And I have never heard from him since. I hope that this may serve as a lesson for other gentlemen of the Church, and teach them that ingratitude, contempt and shame are usually the repercussions for their scandalous behavior. They have to be constantly on their guard and be very careful in their behavior if they want to command respect. It has become fairly well known that purity of morals and a virtuous way of life do not depend at all upon the clothes that are worn, and that the passions of lust rage with equal strength under the robes of the inhabitants of a monastery as they do in the trousers of worldly men. But a man of the world can do things which a priest cannot get away with. The latter is bound to a moral standard of living from which the other is allowed a certain freedom. It is the duty of a priest to at least keep up the pretense. He will have to hide his lusts and desires under a mask of virtue and devotion. It is his main duty to attract the attention of the others by going through the motions of the tenets of Christianity. These duties should take up all of his time and it would be impossible to expect more from him since that would be opposing the demands of Nature. It is up to Her and not to him to work miracles. The man of the Church must also avoid, at any and all cost, laying himself open to ridicule. In all his public dealings he should behave himself as if he had the entire situation under control. After all, that is what he gets paid for. And now, let us leave him in peace.

# CHAPTER FIFTEEN. *MYLORD*

The painful memories of my charitable act toward the abbe caused me to be even more careful with my health. I followed my doctor's orders very conscientiously and soon I was able to contract a new alliance. I did not wait long.

A terribly rich man, or rather a terrible man who was very rich, offered me his golden respect and sterling love. He was a small, dumpy individual with a figure like a big toe, who waddled like a duck, constantly bothered by a Catalan sword which always seemed to be in the way, and a heavy sword-knot which dangled practically down to his ankles. His mental capacity matched his physical looks so perfectly that it would have been very embarrassing to be put to the task of finding out which one was the more preferable—they were created to go together. Maybe, dear reader, you ask yourself why there were so many freak creatures among my chosen ones? But don't forget that good-looking people are not always the richest, nor are they the ones who seek out a love affair with us. Among the ones who seek us out are idiots, blockheads and ugly faces with so much money they don't know what to do with it. And above all, you should never forget that we are only interested in our personal gain and that a poodle or a monkey with a well-filled purse stands a better chance for a loving reception than the most handsome cavalier in the world without one. That is the powerful magic of money which causes us to be on the lookout for personal gains and for those who are able to afford this.

The guineas of Mylord had changed his personality as far as I was concerned, because in my eyes he was a veritable knight in shining armor. He did cause me to change my way of life in a most peculiar manner, as long as he had the honor of sharing his income with me. More than half the time we ate grilled pieces of beef, lamb chops and veal (dripping in butter), covered with cabbage leaves with which one usually feeds the livestock in the barnyard. Often (and it had to be his favorite food) we would have a chunk of pig with mashed potatoes. His taste for drink was equally as exquisite. Burgundy and the best French wines caused him heartburn. He insisted upon a drink which irritated and scratched the throat, the type which the lowliest towncriers used. And it should be obvious that neither punch (made out of brandy, lemons, sugar and water!) nor pipe tobacco was left out of the picture. When Mylord had loaded himself with these ghastly mixtures and gorged himself to his heart's content, he would burp like a pig, put his feet up on the table and fall asleep. I would not have liked getting used to these barbarous customs were it not for the fact that I made a considerable fortune out of it. Though Mylord was everything but generous, I always managed to wrangle out of him whatever I needed. All I had to do was to blacken my countrymen, drink a toast to King George, and wish the Pope and the Dauphin to the devil. With the help of these small attentions I acquired the liberty of emptying his pockets. One day I made as much as three hundred *louis d'or* simply with a few short toast speeches. I told him that I wanted the most fantastic *deshabille* made for me that I could think of, and also that his incredible good taste had won renown all over Paris. I sweetly asked him if he would care to escort me to a little shop in the *rue Saint-Honore*.

"But naturally, my dear," answered Mylord. "That is how it should be. Yes, yes! Very well. That is a jolly good idea. Extremely good. My opinion shall be very valuable. By God, I can tell at first glance what will look good on you."

You will never guess what I succeeded in getting out of him on that little trip: two bales of cloth, each thirty yards long; the first one of silver *lame* for a short housecoat, and the other one of gold for the trimmings. But that is nothing compared to some other expenses which I managed to get him to pay for me. All I had to do was tell him about some generosity of one of my previous admirers and he would immediately and jealously do anything in his power to go them one better. He simply could not stand the implication that there would be a mortal on earth more generous than a peer of Great Britain. His stupid pride earned me in less than four months five thousand pounds sterling in solid coin and at least as much in jewelry and gowns.

Even though Mylord made himself extremely unpopular whenever he went with his boorish manners, he still managed to have a very high opinion of his massive personality. He insisted that there was not a man in all of France who was stronger, braver and more gallant than he. Jumping, fighting, any choice of weapons, dancing and horseback riding—he was able to do all of these equally well, and in his opinion it was simply ridiculous not to be able to master all of these fine arts. He often amused himself in my home fighting Monsieur de Gr . . . M . . . with rapiers. The latter delivered blows in cold blood that would have killed an ox. Mylord took them stoically as if he had not ever been touched.

To avoid any further arguments, the gentlemen agreed one evening to paint the points of their rapiers. After this agreement, Monsieur de Gr ... M ... mixed some soot from the chimney with oil and made some kind of ointment out of it with which each of the gentlemen rubbed the tip of his weapon. Immediately after that both gentlemen started to stab at each other and suddenly Mylord was hit smack on his stomach. He could hardly deny it because the black spot on his *jabot* was ample proof that a serious duel would have been very fatal for him. He satisfied himself with the explanation that he had not carried his weapon high enough. But, since in reality he was out of his mind with barely suppressed fury, he suddenly thrust his rapier at Monsieur de Gr . . . M . . . with a graceless gesture, his mouth wide open. The latter, who had finally lost some of his infinite patience, parried with a counter-thrust and his rapier got stuck in Mylord's throat. Aside from the unfortunate fact that he started to spit blood which was as black as that of the medusa, Mylord also had the bad luck to spit out two of his best teeth. Nevertheless there was nothing I could do to change his high opinion of himself or to make him abstain from showing off his courage. And since he was firmly convinced that I admired him greatly, it did not take him long ere he had found another way to impress us with his talents. He soon gave us the opportunity to witness the following ridiculous and silly scene.

We were making a trip in an open hansom through the *Bois de Boulogne*. Mylord, who cherished the noble desire to show us his adroitness in driving a carriage, told the coachman to take a seat in the hansom while he swung himself upon the box. As long as the terrain remained even and flat, without any deep furrows or other—similar—obstacles, everything went smoothly. But when he succeeded in driving us at a most inopportune moment into a narrow pass, he needed all his dexterity to avoid a collision with a carriage that came speeding from the opposite direction. The sudden brainpower required for this unexpected emergency and the quick decisions he had to make during this maneuver, made him forget that he was talking English to the horses! And, unfortunately for him, they were well-trained coach horses not used to any freedom. They heard a lot of strange sounds which they did not comprehend and consequently they did exactly the opposite of what he had commanded them to do. Without hesitating the stupid animals jumped the oncoming *equipage* and became entangled in its wheels. The other coachman did not expect Mylord to be anything else but some miserable pupil of the carriage drivers' trade and, in accordance with their habits, he dealt him such a blow with his whip that My-lord fell off his coach box. Our Phaethon, who was furious about his fall and even more incensed about the unexpected caress, promptly threw off his wig and top coat and assumed a fighting stance, challenging the robust fellow. That strong and muscular man took him up on his charges. However, Mylord, as unafraid as Mars, stood there—one foot in front of the other, his fists crossed—ready to defend himself. His opponent, who was not used to elegant refinements, wanted to start the attack by hitting Mylord over the head. But his blow was warded off and countered by a thwack across the mouth, followed by a second and third of equal strength. This manner of fighting, to which the Frenchman was unaccustomed, unnerved him completely, made him shake convulsively, lose his equilibrium, and fall over backward. After he had rubbed the cartilage in his nose and wiped the dust out of his mustache, the coachman got up, ready for murderous revenge. Our British hero assumed his fighting stance again, steady as a rock, and ready to bash in that stupid skull or to batter one eye or both, when the Frenchman kicked him completely unexpectedly—and forcefully—in the belly. Mylord was stretched out cold like a banged-up frog. He got up from the battlefield, groaning, and cried something like "that kick was a bloody rum show." He insisted that we hand him his rapier, so that he could pierce the traitor's belly. We considered his howling and wailing rather childish, since in our opinion that kick was about as good a kick as any we had ever seen. After he had calmed down a little, Mylord finally enlightened us by explaining that kicking is absolutely out of order in the noble sport of boxing. We ultimately succeeded in quieting him down completely by explaining to him that these noble rules were totally unknown in France, and that it had simply never occurred to us that it might be unmannerly to make use of all four of our limbs if the circumstances warrant such a defense. Fully satisfied with our clever explanation, Mylord climbed back upon his box, and was barely able to suppress his delight about the shining victory he had just won. He really filled his onlookers with admiration; the art of getting into fisticuffs is a natural talent with the English and their country has produced without a doubt some of the most famous men in this field.

Not long after these martial adventures, domestic problems recalled Mylord to England. And since he did not doubt that the thought of having to lose him distressed me extremely, he assured me—to console me and to flatter his self-love—that he hated to leave Paris for two reasons only: me, and the bullfights.

# CHAPTER SIXTEEN. *THE TAX COLLEC-TOR*

When Mylord departed I was in the possession of a rather great capital and I could have led a life of leisure, keeping up my estate, for the rest of my days. But I have discovered that the desire for more increases relative to our gains and that avarice and frugality are the constant companions of abundance and wealth. The passion for comfort and the hope of even more complete satisfaction shortens the time we could take out for indulgence. Our necessities multiply as fast as our income grows. And even while wallowing in opulence we are constantly afraid of having to suffer privation. My income was over twelve thousand pounds but I did not dare to think about retirement ere I had reached an annuity of twenty thousand. It is true, that a girl as highly desirable as I should not exceed the bounds of possibility which fate erects. However, the next act of favor which it dropped into my lap proved to me that my ambitions were well within the limits of workability. As a matter of fact, my Englishman could not have yet reached Dover when a member of the Academy of Forty from the *Hotel des Fermes* showed up to replace him. I received him with all the outward signs of esteem and consideration his money vault demanded. Nevertheless, without being blinded by the honors he paid me, I told him that I preferred connections with foreigners and I could only accept his kind offer under the condition that our contract would be null and void the very moment I could attract a gentleman from abroad. He agreed to this and we sealed our covenant.

He was a rather strong, straight and tall man who was not too bad looking. Otherwise he was an utterly unbearable fellow, as often happens to people in his position. The world was without bounds, except, of course, for his own person. He considered himself a universal genius and his every decision was a final one. He disagreed with anyone and everything, but woe to the person who did not concur with his opinions. He insisted that people listen to him, without ever deigning to hear the views of anyone else. Briefly, this conceited nuisance would happily cut the throat of any decent person and then expect loud and happy approval of his poor victims and their friends.

The best thing he did after entering my home was to restore the results of Mylord's bad taste and institute in its stead the luxury which is considered normal among people of considerable financial wealth. Every noon and every evening my table was laid for eight persons; six places were always occupied by poets, musicians and painters. In the interest of their bellies they squandered their corruptible incense, like slaves, on my Croesus. My home was a tribunal where talent and the arts were judged with the same superiority as in the literary saloon of Madame T .... All the good authors were run down and hacked to pieces with a smile, just as at her place. Only the bad ones found favor in their eyes; yes, those were veritably placed on a pedestal. I have heard this rabble degrade the incomparable letters written by the author of *"The Temple of Cnidus."* They even threw stink-bombs, as it were, at the respectable Abbe Pellegrin to support their opinion that his *"Lettres Juifs"* was merely a jumble of ideas, taken from *"Baby-lone,"* the *"Bibliotheque universelle du Clerc,"* even from *"L'espion turc"* and many other works. Every single idea was supposedly horribly maimed and each one of the mangled sentences betrayed the Provencal language. This poor priest, whose only disadvantages were his extreme destitution and his uncleanliness, but whose slovenly body enveloped a beautiful soul—this hapless man who has always been the butt of unwarranted sarcasms—possessed an excellent power of judgment. I must admit to his credit that, if I have any taste for the good things in life at all and if I know how to protect myself from the contagious fever of pretension to wit and culture, it is only because I have tried to follow his outstanding advice. It was he who opened my eyes about the small and transitory value of our drones of Parnassus and who made me aware that true intelligence and imagination are a pure, divine fire, a gift from Heaven, and that it is not within the power of Man to acquire it. It is very important not to confuse this prophetic genius, who is impelled by divine ardor, with the despicable multitude of quill-drivers who color their scribblings with so-called aesthetic assumed names. Those nicknames are now considered a disgrace by decent people, and even though the confessions laid down in Pellegrin's letters belong to the most noble works in literature, one feels embarrassed to support them because of the bad name this legion of vermin has given to letter-writing in our society.

"You could hardly guess," he said to me one day, "why Paris has been infected with this accursed rabble. It is simply because this trade requires neither talent nor brains. If you want to convince yourself, just teach your coachman a dozen words from the newly published encyclopedia and send him for one or two months to the *Cafe Procope.* I guarantee you that, upon his return, he will be as much a literary wit as the others. Aah," he added with a deep sigh, "I owe all the misery and ridicule which has been heaped upon my head for such a long time to the cruelty of my own family. These barbarous people forced me to enter this order when I was still a youngster. My initial opposition against the monastic class grew stronger when I became older. I have lamented many a year since I was forced to don the cowl and I would have died of frustration if it had not been for my discovery of a way to secularize. But, without friends, without money, and stripped bare of almost everything, my freedom soon became a burden to me. I had almost reached the point where I started to yearn for the fetters that had

**91**

been strangling me. And, since I did not know where to go, my indecision led me to come here. In the beginning I managed to make ends meet with the proceeds of my celebrations of the Mass and the writing of sermons which I used to sell to other mendicant friars. My misery and inaction did not permit me to be too squeamish in the selection of my acquaintanceships. I frequented a small tobacco parlor near the market place of *Saint-Germain* where tightrope walkers, puppeteers, a few mimics from the *Opera comique,* and—among others—Monsieur Colin, the well-known candle cleaner of the *Comedie francaise,* used to get together. I was lucky enough to be liked by these gentlemen, and they gave me tickets to watch their performances. Soon an inordinate desire to scribble upon paper overwhelmed me. I risked my chances and tried my hand at a few bad scenes, and was ridiculously overpaid for them. I would have preferred to make my peace with both the Church *and* the Theater so that I could still cash in on my daily tributes to the altar. However, the bishop decided to rob me of this small but regular income by forbidding me to function as a preacher and I lost fifteen *sous* daily which were the proceeds of my Masses and my only true means of support. So, in order to compensate for this loss, I decided to become a professional poet and I started to put together comedies, operas and tragedies which I succeeded to have performed under the name of my brother, the cavalier. Or, I sold them to just about anybody who had the desire to become known as an author. Aside from that I traded wholesale and retail in everything that belongs to the domain of the mind. Whoever wanted a poem to go with a bouquet of flowers, or a verse to brighten weddings, or a spiritual song, or sermons for lent; he could find them all—and at favorable prices—in my repository. I count upon your honor to remain silent about this, but many an honored member of this Society of Promiscuous Chatterboxes in the Louvre has not found it beneath his dignity to seek refuge with me and beg me to write his speech of acceptance. Who would not believe that such a thriving business nevertheless did not even permit me to own at least a carriage? But I ask you to judge for yourself about the gains I have made. Look at me. I have composed millions of poems during the past fifty years, and I do not even own a pair of trousers."

The candid and naive manner in which this good man expressed himself convinced me that of all the professions that of a literary wit was the most thankless and thoughtless one, but the true merits of the man also assured me that literature, like any other profession, has its share of fortunate people and that there exists a considerable number of authors who earned their fame and reputation more thanks to their lucky stars than with the help of their talents. Oh, how many false celebrities have I known in Paris about whom not a single soul would have ever heard were it not for the protection of some influential personage at Court or for a whore who vouchsafed for his credit and good standing. I know of so many who are considered high-ranking pupils of Apollo thanks to the aforementioned authorities, and who would never be capable of milking the sterile brains for just a mere fraction of the brilliant ideas that flowed out of the mind of the good Abbe Pellegrin. I beg indulgence for the odious comparison, but the poor devil reminds me of the Jester at the fairs, generating the mockery and derisive laughter of the common people, and being doomed to remain eternally a plaything for his colleagues, albeit he is fundamentally of far more value than all of them together. We can safely draw the conclusion that any amount of talent is absolutely useless unless it gets help from Fate. It depends upon the circumstances, to create great men; Nature merely supplies ability.

But, let us go back to our great provider, the money man. The authorities had selected him to travel the circuit, which means that he had to see to it that his underlings dealt severely enough with the people in squeezing them dry and robbing them blind, and to find out if any other methods could be applied to milk them for even more. We therefore relinquished our mutual contract while remaining good friends, and I was free once more.

# CHAPTER SEVENTEEN. *A WIDOW AGAIN*

I should have answered a question a long time ago, a question which my readers have undoubtedly asked themselves more than once. How was it possible for Margot, who was obviously born with the temperament of a Messalina, to get any satisfaction out of affairs with people she met only for personal gain and who for the most part were considerably less than Hercules in the art of making love? No question makes more sense and it is only right that I satisfy your curiosity. So it may please you to learn, my dear gentlemen readers, that I had in my service—following the example of the duchesses of the Old Court and many of my own colleagues (but, please, let that remain a secret between us)—a young and strong lackey who made me feel comfortable, so comfortable indeed that, even though at times my conscience bothered me somewhat, I never changed my methods. Aside from the fact that these fellows remain unimportant, they supply their services at an instant's notice and they are never boring like honorable people. And it is also very easy to get rid of them if they become impudent or bold. Just give them a solid whipping, pay them and send them away; that is not difficult at all. Personally I have never had any need for these ultimate measures because I have always been careful to get them fresh from the country. I have the satisfaction of training them myself and bend them according to my own desires. I definitely forbid them to have any contact with their own kind because I am afraid that those fellows could spoil their innocence and divert their attention from the work at hand. I keep them, as it were, on a chain. They are well-kept and fed, like roosters in a hen house; or, to be less descriptive, like those fortunate superiors of the nuns who have no other care in the world than to keep them piously in good condition and surrender unconditionally to whatever else may arise.

There you have it, gentlemen—since you kept insisting—the recipe I use daily to temper the glowing fire of my unfulfilled passions. With the use of this ingenious system, I avoid mixing my pleasures with that certain tinge of bitterness. I take my enjoyment in peace and quiet, without having to be afraid of the caprices and bad temper of some domineering lover who might treat me as his slave, and who could possibly force me to pay him for his caresses out of my hard-earned savings, thus reducing me one of these days to beggary. I do not belong to that breed of common street whores.

It may very well be that those who long for beautiful passion and platonic love can thrive on it; I feed by no means on hot and undulating passions, since pompous and artificial emotions while making love are not the kind of nourishment I consider healthy for my constitution. I need stronger fare. Mister Plato surely was a funny character prescribing his ways of love. What would have happened to the human race if everyone had followed the ruffled train of thought of this spoiler of our profession?

But, let us resume our story.

The news of my widowhood barely had time to spread through Paris, when I was besieged by a throng of new admirers from all classes and of all sorts. It was a special Ambassador who thoroughly liberated me from their molestations. I could not hide my joy of having made such an important conquest. My vanity was flattered enormously. It was an incredible satisfaction to know that I had intrigued and captured a man whose adroitness was able to sway opinions, who could change the entire system of European affairs with the acuteness of his brilliant thoughts and his thorough knowledge of the varied interests of the sovereign and his cabinet, and who could at the same time change everything for the common good and contribute to the greater glory of his country. That was the glorious picture I had in my mind of my new master, the Ambassador, ere I had met him personally. I did not doubt for a moment the existence of a thousand more beautiful characteristics in addition to the rare and outstanding talents I have just mentioned, and it did not dawn on me that one had to have a rather towering personality to be able to fulfill expectations of such magnitude. My high opinion of him was actually strengthened by the rather peculiar manner in which we conducted our transactions. We reached our agreement through negotiations. He sent secret emissaries to me, and I dispatched mine to him. They consulted with one another. They listened to the proposed bids which were carefully checked and debated. Each of the parties tried to make the most of it and thus multiplied the difficulties. Failures and disadvantages were found everywhere, and if there were none, they were created on the spot. Whenever they reached agreement at one point, they created disagreements at the next. After several disrupted and newly appointed conferences our plenipotentiaries finally (and luckily) signed the articles and, after having made out duplicates, we were finally satisfied and exchanged the copies of our contracts.

Since I now have reason to believe that the reader has become impatient, and finally wants to know the name of His Excellency, I will not wait any longer to give you his description.

The Ambassador had one of those faces which could be called insignificant and colorless and which is therefore extremely difficult to describe. His stature was slightly above average, not especially well-built, but not exactly too bad either. Like most people of quality, his legs were rather thin and bony. He carried a certain air of pretension which, however, contrasted unfavorably with his average and mediocre face. He held his chin high and his neck stiff which made his cheeks look rather puffy, and he glanced continuously down upon the many decorations which had been bestowed upon him. To judge by his stern, taciturn and introverted expression, one could conclude that he was continually in deep thought. He hardly ever talked, thus indicating that his mind was preoccupied, and his demeanor made it clear that he was very careful and kept a tight reign on his lips during conversations. Whenever a question was posed he answered with a barely discernible nod which was either accompanied by a secretive glance or an imperceptible smile. Who, then, would not believe that my partiality for the Ambassador should turn into regret in less than one month because of these peculiar airs of distinction and his ambiguous behavior? I could never have been talked out of believing that he was one of the most important personages of our time, were it not for the well-intentioned picture that his secretary drew of him. Earlier I have already stated that we have no more rigorous and unrelenting fault-finders than our own servants. If, despite their ignorance, our faults do not escape them, how could we possibly hope to avoid their sharp tongues when they happen to be intelligent and well-informed? This one was too enlightened to be taken in by the arrogance and forced seriousness of his Lord and Master. No matter whom the servants are talking about, I have always found that their observations are invariably correct, and thus I have decided, dear reader, to let you know what the findings of the Secretary were. This is the extent of what he had to say to me:

"Always remember, so that you may never be disappointed and cheated, that the great ones are only great when compared to our smallness and that a ridiculous bias infuses us with a blind and cowardly respect towards them, which makes them look so tall in our eyes. You just try it; look them straight in the eyes, divest them of the glitter with which they surround themselves, and suddenly their halo of respect and dignity will vanish into thin air. You will instantly recognize their true value and see for yourself that all those things which you had hitherto taken for greatness and dignity turn out to be nothing but arrogance and stupidity.

There is *one* axiom which you should never forget: do not overlook the fact that every personal merit merely matches the importance of the authority with which one has been invested, just as much as the quality of a horse is frequently judged by the costliness of its bridle. However, if you harness an old nag to its best advantage, cover it with a beautiful saddlecloth, put it before the most beautiful and costly carriage, all the adornment and decoration in the world will not change one whit the mere fact that you still have an old nag. In a similar manner, the limited mind of His Excellency cannot grasp the idea that a repelling demeanor, a serious and stereotyped behavior, proud and imperious gestures are the only characteristics necessary to make a minister of the King. Personally I find this the typical behavior of an idiot. He may, for all I care, pretend to be as imposing as he wants, act as if he can hear the grass grow, and puff himself up with the importance of his mission, one will always be able to recognize that, despite his so-called self-control and his exertions, the cross is too weak for such a heavy burden. It will never fail; the moment he is sure that the public eye is no longer upon him, he will unload this burden upon his secretaries. And then, what do you think is going on whilst we sweat and try to decipher his dispatches, groping for appropriate answers? He is playing around with his servants, his monkeys and his dogs. He cuts silhouettes out of newspapers, warbles little songs, plays the flute, falls back into an easy chair, stretches his legs and goes to sleep. I do not want you to think that all of our Ministers cut such a miserable figure. There are some whose services are far greater than all the praises which could be heaped upon them. I knew many of the latter who combined their professional capacities with those that brought them respect and general esteem. Quite contrary to those farcical colleagues who cannot keep up with what is going on in the King's cabinet, but who are kept in high esteem by society because of their craze for amusement. In this respect they are better politicians, since the air of confidence and candor which they seem to ooze causes people to underestimate them and to forget keeping their lips buttoned."

The secretary told me quite a few other excellent things which I am not at liberty to repeat. But since there is nothing which ultimately does not become boring, I would like to try and make my reader's mouth water. The admiration and respect which I had hitherto felt for His Excellency turned soon into disdain. Despite his generosity and his many costly presents, I would have been capable of playing any trick on him in order to regain my freedom, if it had not been for a sudden collapse of my health that gave both of us a perfect reason for a separation.

# CHAPTER EIGHTEEN. *I RETIRE*

I fell into fits of melancholy and tiredness which became dangerous stumbling blocks for the knowledge of all the Aesculapians I consulted. Every single one of them was equally as ignorant about the true suffering which had taken hold of me. Everyone had his own ideas and convinced me with his, alas so forceful, rhetoric, that I firmly believed myself to be suffering from all the ills of the world rolled into one. I eagerly accepted the pills and potions they offered me, and in a very short time my body had become a veritable apothecary. Nevertheless I kept losing weight under their very eyes and soon I was a mere shadow of my former self. I tried in vain to replace the natural freshness of my complexion, my healthy color and my normally voluptuous figure with deceiving secret cosmetics. But the rouge for my cheeks, the salves for my skin, the white powder make-up and the beauty plasters, all of them were incapable of reflecting the pretty face of Margot in my mirror. Despite thorough searching and painfully accurate studies in my looking glass—which sometimes lasted for more than two hours—I could barely find a single familiar line to remind me of the beauty I used to possess. I looked as if I had been prepared for the stage where the magic of distance makes one look desirable but where one cannot bear to be looked at from close by. The various layers of make-up which I had applied to my face gave me at a distance a certain dignity and caused my eyes to sparkle. However, upon closer scrutiny, one discovered merely a large amount of curiously applied harsh colors whose roughness insulted the eye and which made it impossible to discover any similarity with my original looks.

And while I gave in to my misery, following all the prescriptions of my doctors, dragging along in a miserable existence, I finally heard mention of a quack who had acquired the nickname of "Eye-watcher" because he insisted that he was able to diagnose the origin of every ailment by looking into the eyes. Even though I had never put trust in people who carry on their trade in secrecy, the weakness which had befallen me made me impervious to the spirit of disbelief. And since there exists nothing one cannot be talked into, I sent a messenger to "Mister Eye-watcher," begging him to pay me a visit. I liked his physiognomy at first glance. I found myself confronted by an honest and charming face instead of one of those terrifying expressions which are so frequently worn by doctors and charlatans. He began with the request that I tell him briefly but frankly about my way of life up until my illness, as well as about the treatments I had undergone to cure myself. After that, he looked at me carefully for two or three minutes without moving or saying a single word. He then interrupted his silence with the following reassurance:

"Madame, you can consider yourself lucky that your doctors have not actually killed you. Your illness, which they do not understand one iota, is not a disease of the body but a satiation of the soul caused by the excess of voluptuous and luxuriant living. The passions are to the soul what good cookery is to the stomach. The most exquisite meals become stale and commonplace out of habit. They finally frighten us and we are no longer capable of digesting them. The over-abundance of sexual pleasures has, to put it bluntly, over-saturated your heart and deadened your sentiments. Despite the comforts of your present situation, you are no longer capable of appreciating them. Pressing apprehensions haunt you amidst your pleasures and even blissful delights have become a torture unto you. That is the entire situation. If you care to accept my advice, you would flee from the hustle and bustle of society. Use exclusively healthful and nourishing food. Go to bed on time and get up early. Give yourself some exercise, and visit people whose moods are compatible with your own. Find something to do in order to fill the emptiness of your existence. And, especially, do *not* take any medications! I guarantee you that within six weeks you will be as fresh and beautiful as you have ever been." The conversation with "Mister Eye-watcher" made such a fantastic impression upon my senses that I would have thought—if I had believed in witchcraft at all—he had touched me with a magic wand. I felt as if I had awakened from a deep sleep during which I had dreamt that I was terribly ill. I was firmly convinced that "Mister Eye-watcher" had rescued me from the jaws of Death, and in a sudden outburst of gratitude and joy I embraced him fervently and upon his leaving I rewarded him with a suitable gift of twelve *louis d'or.*

Since I was determined to follow his advice rigorously, my first concern was to announce my exit from the *Opera.* Even though one is expected to stay on for another six months after such an announcement, Monsieur Thuret was happy to make an exception in my case. It seemed as if I had time to think. I had never once thought about my parents since the day I had run away from home. It was as if they had never existed, as if I had dropped from Heaven. The change which had come over me, called them back into my thoughts. I reproached myself for this ingratitude and hoped that I could make amends, provided they were both still alive. My searching was fruitless for quite some time. Finally an old peddler in herbs informed me that Monsieur Tranche-montagne had ended his days as a galley slave in Marseille and my mother was at the moment locked up in the *Salpetriere* after she had received a public correction at the hands of Monsieur de Paris.

I was deeply touched by their misfortunes. And it was far from me to reproach their behavior which had caused them their conditions. I could do no more than justify their actions in my heart, because I remembered the sensible reflections of the lawyer Patelin that it is very difficult to remain an honest person when one is poor. Truly there are so many people who behave as if they are integrity incarnate only because they have no wants; they might have committed worse crimes if they had been in a similar situation. As they say, there is only good luck and bad luck in this world. And the ones who have bad luck are hanged. I don't doubt that if everyone who really deserved it would dangle from the end of a rope, our globe would soon be depopulated.

Strengthened by this conviction, whether it is true or not, I used my influence to have my mother released from her imprisonment and I had no doubt that the change of her environment would soon turn her into a respectable woman. Thank God, I was not mistaken. Today she is one of the most sensible and prudent ladies I can think of. She was more than happy to take over the care of my household and I must admit to her honor that nobody has ever taken more interest in my home. In short, if I have done anything at all to contribute to her happiness, she is doing no less for me with her tender love and true eagerness in taking care of everything and anticipating my slightest wishes.

We divide our time between our city and our country homes and enjoy among the pleasures of life only those which are the most blissful and available in great variety.

As far as my health is concerned, except for a little insomnia now and then, it is excellent. But, since "Mister Eye-watcher" positively forbade any form of medicine, I hit upon the idea of reading some passages from the sleep promoting works of the Marquis d'Argens, the Chevalier de Mouhy and many other authors of a similar outstanding nature, and in no time at all I sleep like a top. I advise anybody with similar difficulties to try it and I can give them my word that it is the best remedy.

The only thing which remains now is to answer the accusation that I have been a bit too liberal in certain descriptions. I have been prompted by the following considerations: I firmly believe that the only way to discredit these ladies of pleasure is to paint them in the most repulsive colors and to expose the infamous tricks of their trade. Moreover, whatever the reader may think of it, I flatter myself that the obscene parts of my memoirs are fully justified by the good use which young people, about to enter society, may make of them. Let them know about the artful training of these whores and they can draw their own conclusions about the obvious dangers inherent in visiting them. If I have succeeded, and the results are what I expect them to be—the better for them. If not, I wash my hands in innocence.

THE END

WITHDRAWN
FROM STOCK
QMUL LIBRARY

9 781596 545045